the lily pond

ALSO BY ANNIKA THOR

A Faraway Island

Winner of the Mildred L. Batchelder Award
for an outstanding children's book originally
published in a foreign language

the lily pond

ANNIKA THOR

Translated from the Swedish by Linda Schenck

Delacorte Press

Translation copyright © 2011 by Linda Schenck
Jacket art copyright © 2011 by Juliana Kolesova

All rights reserved. Published in the United States by Delacorte Press,
an imprint of Random House Children's Books, a division of Random House, Inc.,
New York. Originally published in Sweden as
Näckrosdammen by Annika Thor, copyright © 1997 by Annika Thor, by Bonnier
Carlsen, Stockholm, in 1997. This English translation published in arrangement with
Bonnier Group Agency, Stockholm, Sweden.

Delacorte Press is a registered trademark and the
colophon is a trademark of Random House, Inc.

Visit us on the Web! www.randomhouse.com/kids

Educators and librarians, for a variety of teaching tools,
visit us at www.randomhouse.com/teachers

Library of Congress Cataloging-in-Publication Data
Thor, Annika.
[Näckrosdammen. English]
The lily pond / Annika Thor ; translated from the Swedish by Linda Schenck. —1st
American ed.
p. cm.
Sequel to: A faraway island.
Summary: Having left Nazi-occupied Vienna a year ago, thirteen-year-old Jewish
refugee Stephie Steiner adapts to life in the cultured Swedish city of Gothenburg,
where she attends school, falls in love, and worries about her parents who were not
allowed to emigrate.
ISBN 978-0-385-74039-5 (hc) — ISBN 978-0-385-90838-2 (glb) —
ISBN 978-0-375-89914-0 (ebook)
1. World War, 1939–1945—Refugees—Juvenile fiction. [1. World War, 1939–1945—
Refugees—Fiction. 2. Refugees—Fiction. 3. Schools—Fiction. 4. Friendship—Fiction.
5. Jews—Sweden—Fiction. 6. Göteborg (Sweden)—History—20th century—Fiction.
7. Sweden—History—Gustav V, 1907–1950—Fiction.] I. Schenck, Linda. II. Title.
PZ7.T3817Li 2011
[Fic]—dc22
2010053548

The text of this book is set in 12-point Goudy.

Book design by Kenny Holcomb

Printed in the United States of America

10 9 8 7 6 5 4 3 2 1

First American Edition

the lily pond

one

The funnel of the steamboat opens wide, releasing a mournful howl and a cloud of black smoke. The moorings have been dropped, and the gangway has been drawn up. In a wide arc the boat pulls away from the pier and steers out to sea.

Stephie stands in the stern, waving. All the people on the pier wave back: Nellie, Auntie Alma, the little ones, and Vera. Stephie said goodbye to Uncle Evert last night, before he headed off with the fishing boat he works on, the *Diana*. When he and the rest of the crew return with their catch in a few days, Stephie won't be there.

The people on the pier are shrinking; soon Stephie can't see them. The last thing she loses sight of is Vera's copper-red hair, glistening in the sun.

"Let's go inside and sit down," Aunt Märta says. "Our clothes are getting dirty from the coal smoke."

Brushing a few particles of dirt only she can see off the sleeve of her light summer coat, Aunt Märta precedes Stephie to the passenger area, her little straw hat pressed firmly down over the gray bun at her neck.

Aunt Märta's wearing her very best clothes to take Stephie to Göteborg, where Stephie is going to board with Dr. Söderberg and his wife, so she can continue her schooling. The school on the island is only for the first six years. One weekend a month, and on vacations, she'll stay with Aunt Märta and Uncle Evert. It's all planned.

The air in the passenger area is muggy; Stephie fans herself with a newspaper someone left on the bench where they're sitting. Aunt Märta, though, sits straight as a ramrod, with her buttons done up to the neck and the corners of her head scarf crossed neatly over her chest. She doesn't seem to notice the heat.

The suitcase at Stephie's side contains nearly all her earthly possessions: her clothes, her books, her diary, and her photographs of Mamma and Papa. The only thing she left in the room under the eaves at Aunt Märta and Uncle Evert's is her old teddy bear. She's a big girl now, thirteen.

She intends to go by the name of Stephanie at her new school. It sounds romantic and grown up, not childish like her nickname. Sven, the Söderbergs' son, calls her Stephanie. She's looking forward to seeing him again soon.

"My name is Stephanie," she mutters softly to herself.

"What was that?" asks Aunt Märta.

"Nothing."

"There's no need to be nervous," Aunt Märta tells her. "You're just as good as everyone else, remember that. Better, even."

Aunt Märta doesn't easily dish out praise, or flattery, as she calls it. Coming from her, this is an enormous compliment.

"Aunt Märta," Stephie begins.

"Yes?"

"Have you ever regretted taking me in?"

Aunt Märta looks bewildered. "Regretted? Of course not," she says. "We did the right thing. There's no regretting that."

"But I mean have you never wished they had sent you a different child? A nicer one?"

At that, something even more unusual happens. Aunt Märta laughs.

"Oh, my dear girl, you have the strangest ideas! The thought has never so much as entered my mind. I admit that you do foolish things at times, but you've never done anything so bad that both God and I were not prepared to forgive you."

Stephie can't help wondering who is stricter, Aunt Märta or her God. Or do God and Aunt Märta always agree about everything?

The steamboat barrels along between the little islands and skerries. Off in the distance behind them is the horizon.

A year ago Stephie and her younger sister, Nellie, made

this trip in the opposite direction, from Göteborg out to the faraway island; it was the last leg of their long journey from home. Their parents are still in Vienna. The Swedish government agreed to take in Jewish refugee children, but no adults.

When Stephie was sent to the island, she had to leave everything familiar behind and make her way to a foreign country to live with strangers who spoke a language of which she knew not a word. In a letter to her parents, she wrote, *This place is nothing but sea and stones. I can't live here.* She never sent that letter.

This time she's not leaving because anyone is making her; she's leaving of her own free will. She wants to go on with her education, study hard, and go to the university, where she'll become a doctor, like Papa. She's wanted to follow in his footsteps for as long as she can remember. But from the beginning, of course, she expected to do it all at home, in Vienna.

So here she is, breaking away again, this time from Aunt Märta and Uncle Evert; from Vera, the one friend she finally made; and from Nellie, who's going to stay with Auntie Alma and her family on the island. Will Stephie never again feel completely at home anywhere? Will she always be on her way to the next destination?

The boat will soon be in Göteborg. They've left the sea and are making their way through the mouth of the Göta River to the harbor.

"Couldn't we go out on deck now?" Stephie asks. "I'd like to see the city from the water."

"All right," Aunt Märta concedes. "If it means so much to you."

They stand by the guardrail on the right-hand side. On that bank of the river is the city center. The other bank is actually an island, a big one, called Hisingen, where all the shipyards and industries are.

"Look, the Seaman's Wife." Aunt Märta points to a statue of a woman on a very tall column. "She's looking out to sea, waiting for her husband to return."

Although Stephie can't see the statue's face, she imagines that the woman looks like Aunt Märta, with those worry lines she always has on her forehead when Uncle Evert is out at sea. There is a war on, the fishing waters are a minefield, and although Sweden is not one of the countries at war, Swedish fishing and merchant vessels have been blown up.

The boat docks at the pier, which is very long, wide near the shore and narrower farther out in the river. Men in blue overalls are loading barrels and boxes from nearby trucks. Stephie feels a bit dizzy; she hasn't seen so many people in one place for a very long time. Cautiously, suitcase in hand, she makes her way down the gangplank. She and Aunt Märta press through the crowd toward land. Stephie sees a steady stream of traffic; the cars smell nasty to her unaccustomed nose. She takes a big stride from the pier to the cobblestones. It has been a whole year since she set foot on a city street.

two

To reach the center of town, Aunt Märta leads Stephie to what she refers to as the white tram. Stephie thinks it looks blue like all the noisy trams making their way down the main road. But she says nothing, just contents herself with gazing out the window at the tall stone-and-brick buildings, the shop windows, and the shiny cars rolling past.

City memories flood through her. She knows the feeling of running down cobbled streets wet with rain, rushing so as not to be late for school, doing her best not to knock into any of the other people, also in an early-morning hurry. She knows how it feels to stroll lazily along a shopping street, studying the elegant dresses on display. When they were younger, Stephie and her best friend, Evi, would stand in front of the shops, making up endless stories about the beautiful mannequins in the windows.

Göteborg doesn't resemble Vienna, but it's still a city, with all its sounds and rhythms. The sadness and uncertainty Stephie felt a short time ago disperse, replaced by eager anticipation. Here, in this city, anything might happen.

In contrast, and to Stephie's surprise, Aunt Märta seems nervous. Back home on the island, she always knows, beyond the shadow of a doubt, what needs to be done and what is right. Here she looks around uncomfortably, twisting her white summer gloves in her hands. Time after time she consults the directions the doctor's wife gave her. Suddenly she pulls the rope, and the bell up by the driver rings. The tram pulls to a stop, but Aunt Märta finds that she was too early. Embarrassed, she has to explain to the conductor, with all the other passengers staring, that they really wanted the next stop.

When they finally disembark on a platform in the middle of the wide street, Aunt Märta looks carefully right, left, and then right again before they cross. They turn off the wide avenue, with its rows of planted trees, onto a side street. A couple of blocks later, they turn another corner.

"Here we are," says Aunt Märta.

In front of them stands a four-story yellow brick building. The bricks around the windows are laid out in intricate patterns; the balconies have wrought-iron guardrails. Across the street is a park, a little slope that was spared when the whole area was flattened for housing. Narrow paths lead up among the trees, and the grass is bright green.

Ages ago, in Vienna, before the Germans invaded, Stephie lived across the street from a park—a park with a Ferris wheel.

Aunt Märta nods. "Yes, this is it."

Instead of walking up to the door, Aunt Märta seems to be going back to the corner they came from. Stephie sets her suitcase down, waiting.

"Come along," says Aunt Märta.

"But . . ."

Aunt Märta's not listening. She continues around the corner, through an open gateway and into a courtyard. There is a harsh smell coming from rubbish bins standing off to the side, by a shed.

In the courtyard there are several narrow doors opening onto stairways.

Looking around, Aunt Märta decides which door they will go through. Stephie follows.

Stephie drags her suitcase up four cramped flights of stairs. She has no idea what they're doing, but can sense that no good would come of asking. Finally they stand in front of a tall, narrow door with an enamel plate on it. It reads SÖDERBERG, KITCHEN ENTRANCE.

Aunt Märta rings the bell. A moment later a woman in an apron opens the door. It's Elna, the Söderbergs' maid. She was with them last summer when the family rented Aunt

Märta and Uncle Evert's house on the island. Elna slept on the wooden settle in Aunt Märta's kitchen.

"Good day to you," she says. "Come in. I'll let the mistress know you've arrived." They wait in the large high-ceilinged kitchen. On the wall near the upper part of the door are a bell and a panel with nine little windows. One is open, displaying the number five. As Elna passes, she presses a button and the window with the five shuts.

Stephie's curiosity makes her want to go right over and press the button to see what will happen, but she feels too timid. Besides, it would be childish. Only kids touch everything in sight.

Mrs. Söderberg appears at the kitchen door, smiling.

"Oh, Mrs. Jansson," she exclaims, "there was no need to use the kitchen entrance! My word, walking up all those flights for no reason when we have an elevator!"

Aunt Märta doesn't reply to these apologies; she just extends a hand in formal greeting.

"And little Stephie," the doctor's wife continues in the same effusive tone. "I'm so pleased to see you here."

Stephie curtsies and shakes Mrs. Söderberg's hand.

"Let me show you the room," the doctor's wife says. "This way!"

The kitchen door opens onto a passage so narrow that they have to walk single file. At the end of the hall is another door, this one with a pane of glass, which opens onto the main entrance and foyer, with elegant rugs on the floor.

To the right there is an open double door, and through it Stephie sees a large room full of antique furniture. On the other side is an ordinary door, and a little way along is another. Mrs. Söderberg opens the first of the two doors.

"Here we go!" she says.

The room is beautiful, spacious and bright, with a large window extending from the level of Stephie's waist all the way up to the ceiling. There's a white desk under the window. In fact all the furniture is white: the dresser, the chairs, the bookshelf, the little mirrored dressing table, the bed, with its frilly pink bedspread. The wallpaper is patterned, pink rosebuds against a pale gray background. The tied-back curtains are ruffled and white. There is a little pink-shaded lamp on the dressing table.

"Isn't it the perfect room for a girl?" Mrs. Söderberg asks. "It's just as it was when Karin lived here."

Karin is the daughter in the family, Sven's older sister.

"Karin and Olle are honeymooning in Båstad," Mrs. Söderberg adds. "Sadly, what with the war, they couldn't possibly go abroad. This war is a hardship for us all. You cannot imagine, Mrs. Jansson, what trouble I had arranging the food for their wedding dinner. Rationing! Such a test of our housewifely skills, don't you agree?"

Aunt Märta mumbles some kind of assent. She seems to feel awkward.

"Perhaps you see things differently," the doctor's wife goes on. "I've heard fishermen have never had it so good."

At that, Aunt Märta looks her straight in the eye. "Oh,

yes, at peril to their lives," she replies. "The seabed is full of mines."

Now it's Mrs. Söderberg's turn to mutter, this time an apology. A moment later she's back in form, showing Stephie the closet in one corner of the room and the little cubbyhole with a sink on the other side.

"So you can take all the time you need getting yourself ready in the mornings," she says. "There's a bathroom and toilet at the far end of the hall, too, down toward the kitchen."

In addition to the door to the hallway, there's another door in the room.

"Where does that one go?" Stephie can't help asking.

"To Sven's room," Mrs. Söderberg answers. "And now," she goes on, turning to Aunt Märta, "I think we ought to let little Stephie unpack her things while we have a chat in the library."

Stephie finds herself alone in the room—a room that adjoins Sven's. So close she'll be able to hear him get up in the morning, wash, and take a clean shirt from his closet, maybe whistling to himself.

Right now, though, it's silent on the other side of the wall. He must not be home or he would have come in and said hello. Stephie opens her suitcase and begins to organize her belongings. Her dresses come nowhere near to filling the spacious closet. She thinks about Karin, how she must have had lots of clothes. Not even the dresser is more than half full when Stephie has unpacked. Although there are some books in the bookcase, there is still more than enough room for hers.

She sets her jewelry box with the little twirling ballerina on the dressing table, in front of the mirror. When she opens the drawer to put her comb, brush, and barrettes away, she finds a note.

> Hello, Stephanie,
>
> I'm glad you're here and hope you will like living with all Karin's ruffles and frills. I'm hiking in the mountains. I'll be back Sunday. See you!
>
> Sven

Stephie reads this short message over and over, then folds it carefully and inserts it between the pages of her diary.

When Aunt Märta's ready to leave, Stephie walks her to the door.

"Take care," Aunt Märta says to Stephie. "Keep your clothes neat and clean, and remember your laundry when you come home. Do your best at school and try not to be any trouble to the doctor and his wife."

"Say hello to Uncle Evert from me," Stephie says.

As she's walking out the door, Aunt Märta turns to Stephie and gives her a long look.

For just an instant her voice softens. "Goodbye, dear child," she says. Then she opens the gate to the elevator. The last thing Stephie sees is Aunt Märta's straw hat, going down.

three

What had Stephie imagined, really? That she would be like a new daughter in the Söderberg family? That Dr. Söderberg would invite her into his study after dinner and read aloud to her or challenge her to a game of chess, like Papa used to? That the doctor's wife would tuck her in at night, like Mamma?

If she had any such expectations, she was very wrong. In the Söderberg home, she is a boarder, not a member of the family.

◊　◊　◊

The first evening Stephie is invited into the dining room for dinner with the doctor and his wife. The doctor asks a few distracted questions about Stephie's parents in Vienna and her father's work. Stephie tells him how the Germans forced Papa to close down his private practice two years ago. Now he works at the Jewish hospital, where the patients are dying for want of medicines.

At that, Dr. Söderberg looks uncomfortable and changes the subject, turning to his wife and complaining about the new nurse in his office.

"She pays no attention to detail," he grumbles. Stephie soon stops listening and finishes her dinner in silence.

After dinner, when Mrs. Söderberg has told Elna she can serve the coffee in the parlor, she turns to Stephie.

"Good night, dear," she says.

Obviously, she doesn't want Stephie to spend the evening with them. Stephie mumbles good night, thanks them for dinner, and withdraws to her room.

Something is bothering her. Where is Putte, the family dog, whom she got to walk so often last summer that he almost felt like her own? What if he's gone to live with Karin and Olle? As soon as the possibility crosses her mind, she's so upset she nearly starts to cry. If Putte had been here, he could have slept on her bed.

◊   ◊   ◊

The next morning Stephie wakes up early. It's Sunday, and silence reigns outside her closed bedroom door. She'd like to get up and use the bathroom, but until she knows that the doctor and his wife are up, she doesn't dare. Around nine she hears the front door close and tiptoes down the hall to the bathroom at the far end. Afterward, she heads toward the only open door; it leads to the kitchen, where Stephie finds Elna preparing a breakfast tray. Elna tells her that Mrs. Söderberg always breakfasts in bed, and that on Sundays the doctor goes for a morning walk and has only coffee when he comes back. He never eats anything before lunch, Elna explains to Stephie.

"How about you? Are you hungry?"

Stephie nods.

"Sit down here, and I'll get you something once I've taken the tray in."

When she returns, Elna gives Stephie a cup of tea and a cheese sandwich and has a cup of coffee herself. Elna shows her the bread box, and where the butter and cheese are kept in the pantry, a big walk-in cupboard. Starting tomorrow, Stephie is supposed to make her own breakfast and her lunch sandwiches for school, Elna tells her. And she's to have dinner with Elna in the kitchen, unless Mrs. Söderberg gives other instructions.

"Who's paying your way, your parents?" Elna asks curiously. "Do they send money from abroad?"

Stephie blushes. No, her parents have no money to send. Everything they had is gone, confiscated by the Nazis. Her beautiful, elegant mamma is now someone's maid, just like

Elna. But she doesn't say any of this out loud. And she doesn't tell Elna that some of the money Aunt Märta and Uncle Evert are paying the Söderbergs for her room and board comes from the Swedish relief committee; they took up a charity collection on her behalf. She doesn't even say she's been awarded a scholarship for "gifted girls of little means" to pay for her schoolbooks.

All she says is "My foster parents."

Stephie spends the whole long Sunday in her room while the sun shines outside her tall window. Everything is unfamiliar. Her window looks out not onto the park, but onto the courtyard with the rubbish bins and the shed. A high wall separates their courtyard from the one next door, with rubbish bins and a shed of its own. The only difference she can see is that there is a green bush in one corner of the next courtyard. She could, of course, have taken a walk in the park, but to do that, she would have had either to ask for a key or ring the doorbell to get back in. She doesn't want to trouble Elna unnecessarily. Not to mention that Sven might come home at any time, and she wants to be there when he does. She wishes she had asked Elna when he was expected.

Two little girls are playing in the courtyard. They must be about Nellie's age, around eight. One of them looks a little like her, although she has light brown braids, not black as soot, like Nellie's.

Stephie no longer has braids. Since she cut off her long hair last year, it hasn't grown back like it should. It won't get really long, and it's straggly, so before they left for Göteborg, she asked Aunt Märta to give her a haircut. Now her hair ends even with her chin, with a side part. It makes her look older.

On the other side of her closed door, she hears noises. The front door opens and shuts when Dr. Söderberg comes in from his walk. He starts talking to his wife, though Stephie can't make out the words. She can hear Elna working in the kitchen, and the toilet flushing. The telephone rings once, and Mrs. Söderberg has a long conversation.

The sounds don't seem real. It's as if they have nothing to do with her. In her room, time stands still. She listens to water running in the pipes. Finally, as the afternoon draws to a close, Elna knocks on her door and says it's time for dinner.

"Didn't you have anything better to do than spend such a beautiful day inside?" she asks. "If I'd been free, you wouldn't have caught me sitting staring into thin air like that."

The doctor and his wife have already had their Sunday meal in the dining room, even though Sven hasn't yet come home. He was supposed to return by dinnertime, Elna tells Stephie, and Mrs. Söderberg changed her mind back and forth before deciding they would go ahead without him. She finally gave in when the doctor said that all the military transports on the railway might mean Sven would be delayed for hours. The kitchen is hot and Elna is grumpy. She bangs down the platters and almost whisks Stephie's plate

out from under her nose before she's finished. Elna is supposed to have Sunday evenings off, but now she can't leave
until Sven has come home and had his dinner.

Stephie thinks Elna must have a gentleman friend waiting for her; that must be what's making her so impatient.
Just as impatient as Stephie feels waiting to see Sven again.

four

As Stephie and Elna are eating a gooseberry compote for dessert, there is a sudden commotion at the other end of the apartment. Footsteps, banging, voices.

The next instant something brown and white shoots down the narrow passage and into the kitchen. Stephie slides off her chair and bends toward the floor. Crouching, she opens her arms wide.

"Putte," she whispers into the dog's white fur, then into his ear. "Putte, Putte, Putte."

Putte sets his paws on Stephie's shoulders, licking her cheeks and nose. Elna watches disapprovingly.

"That dog's not supposed to be in the kitchen," she starts.

Before she can go on, Sven fills the kitchen doorway.

"Stephanie!"

Sven is even more suntanned than when he was vacationing on the island. His brown hair has grown; it hangs in his eyes. He's wearing hiking pants, a plaid shirt, and heavy boots. When she sees him, her insides go all warm.

"Sven, would you please remove that dog?" Elna asks. Then she falls silent, glaring at the floor around Sven's feet. Stephie's gaze follows hers, and she sees all the mud and clay he's brought in on his hiking boots. And not just here, of course, but all the way through the apartment.

"Don't be angry, Elna," Sven cajoles. "I'll sweep it up. I wasn't thinking. I'm really sorry."

Elna smiles at that, and Stephie can see she finds it difficult to be mad at Sven for long.

Sven takes Putte by the collar.

"Coming with me?" he asks Stephie.

Then he notices that she was eating dessert.

"Dinner in the kitchen? Why didn't you eat with Mother and Father?"

Elna answers first. "Mrs. Söderberg thought it best so."

Sven's gray eyes narrow for a moment, and his jaw muscles stiffen. Then he laughs and settles in at the kitchen table, too.

"All right, I'll have my dinner here as well, then. That is, Elna, if there's anything left for me."

Elna hurries to set out a plate, a glass, and cutlery and to heat up the leftover Sunday roast.

"When did you arrive?" Sven asks.

"Yesterday."

"Alone?"

"Aunt Märta came along."

Their words come out one by one, like drops from a dripping faucet. It's as if they have become shy with each other, not having seen each other for so long.

When Sven and his family rented Aunt Märta and Uncle Evert's house on the island over the summer, she and Sven weren't bashful. Sven is five years her senior, but he always treated Stephie as his equal. They took Putte for long walks and talked about everything: books they had read, the war, the future.

In spite of his parents' wishes that he become a doctor or a lawyer, Sven is planning to be a writer. One time he read Stephie a short story he'd written. It was about a young man who volunteered for the Spanish Civil War, to fight for freedom and democracy. The story wasn't actually about the soldier, but about his younger brother, who wasn't old enough to go along. The story described the younger brother's feelings when he finally heard the news that his brother had been killed. Stephie thought the story was good, though she couldn't imagine why anyone would volunteer for a war.

And now they're sitting at the kitchen table, being shy with each other. Sven eats his roast veal, potatoes, gravy, and cucumber salad. Stephie pokes at her gooseberry compote. Elna has shut Putte out of the kitchen and is sweeping up the mess on the floor.

Mrs. Söderberg comes into the kitchen.

"Goodness, Sven. Why are you sitting in here?" she asks, startled.

"Did you think I'd have dinner by myself in the dining room?" he asks back. "You've already eaten."

"All right," says his mother. "When you're finished, change your clothes. We're going to the station to pick up Karin and Olle. Father promised them a lift to their new apartment, since they have so much luggage."

"You go ahead," says Sven. "I think I'll take Stephanie for a walk and show her the way to her new school."

His mother opens her mouth to protest, but Sven is faster.

"How is she supposed to find it in the morning otherwise?" he asks. "Are you going to walk her there? Is Elna? I won't have time. I start at eight myself."

"I see. You can't be bothered to welcome your sister back," his mother says, but her tone makes it clear she has abandoned the fight.

"Don't mope, Mamma," says Sven. "We'll walk Putte at the same time so no one will have to do it later."

When his mother has left the kitchen, Sven says, "Families are all right, but I prefer them in small doses. I'll have a shower and change my clothes, and we'll leave in half an hour. Okay?"

Stephie nods. She helps Elna clean up the kitchen when Sven vanishes to the bathroom. Then she waits in her room. She hears Sven pass by in the hall, whistling. A few minutes later there's a knock on the door between their rooms.

"Ready?"

With Putte trailing his leash, they run down the four flights of stairs. Putte's so eager to get out that he beats them to the door, then stands there glaring as if to ask what took them so long.

Once they're outside, Sven turns left from the doorway, and shortly left again. This brings them down to the wide tree-lined avenue, but not at the same spot where Stephie and Aunt Märta got off the tram yesterday.

In front of them is an open square with yellow brick buildings on three sides. They're all very modern, with shiny glass-and-chrome details on the facades. A fountain—at the center of which is a statue of a huge man with seaweed in his hair, surrounded by fish and sea creatures—sits in the middle of the square.

"That's Poseidon," says Sven. "The Greek god of the sea. This square is called Götaplatsen."

He tells her about the buildings: "That one's the city theater, that one's the art museum, and that's the concert hall."

How strange, Stephie thinks, *that they're all new*. In Vienna theaters and museums are housed in ancient buildings with columns and huge entryways, domes and sculptured figures.

They cross Götaplatsen and turn down a narrow pathway between the theater and the steps leading up to the art museum.

"There you are," Sven says, pointing. "That's the Girls' Grammar School."

"Wow."

"Better than the prison I go to, that's for sure," says Sven. "I'll take you there another time. Come on, let's bring Putte over by the lily pond, where he can run around awhile."

They walk on past the school, and soon they arrive at a small pond with a little sandy bank and dark, still water. In the middle there are white water lilies, and farther out a few red ones. Swans and ducks swim among the flowers, and weeping willows hang out over the water, which reflects them. On the far side Stephie can see a lawn and a large brick mansion covered in ivy. It looks like something out of a fairy tale.

Stephie and Sven walk along the water's edge until they come to a bench under a tree. They sit down, and Sven lets Putte off the leash.

"Nervous about starting school?" asks Sven.

"A bit."

"No need," he replies. "I swear you're going to be the smartest girl in the class. If you ask me, though, don't worry about grades. Just focus on what you think will be most useful to you in life. That's the most important thing."

Stephie knows he's right, but she also knows that only top grades will ensure her a continued scholarship, without which Aunt Märta and Uncle Evert won't be able to keep her in school. She has to do well.

"One thing," says Sven. "I don't know what it's going to be like at your school, but at mine there are teachers who favor the new German order and who wouldn't mind seeing it introduced in Sweden. Watch out for those teachers. Don't let them snare you into a trap. And if anybody treats you badly, just tell me about it."

Stephie can't help giggling. "What would you do if I did?"

Sven chuckles, too. "Come galloping on my white stallion to rescue you from the dragon, of course." he says. He stands up. "Come on, time to head home."

While Sven is putting Putte on the leash, Stephie stares out across the dark and mysterious water of the lily pond. This is a place she plans to return to, often.

five

The clock on the yellow brick school building reads ten to nine the next morning when Stephie arrives. The Swedish flag is flying and the schoolyard is full of girls. The youngest ones are her age; the older ones look like young ladies, in their skirts with matching jackets and hats.

Nobody is playing here, as the children did on the island schoolyard. Just a couple of the younger girls are throwing a ball against one of the walls, but very quietly. Most girls are walking around arm in arm or standing in clusters chatting. Some, like Stephie, are all alone.

She catches a glimpse of Sylvia, the daughter of the shopkeeper on the island, who was in Stephie's class there. She's with Ingrid, another of their old classmates. They don't notice Stephie, and she doesn't call out to them.

◇　◇　◇

Stephie was right last evening when she guessed that the tall windows in the upper floor of the annex belonged to the auditorium. Now the girls all go in and sit in the wooden seats on either side of the aisle. The principal welcomes them to a new school year. The school chorus sings. Then the girls' names are called, along with their assigned classes.

"Stephanie Steiner?"

"Present."

Stephie is going to be in 1A; Sylvia and Ingrid, in 1B. That's a relief. It's not that Sylvia intimidates her the way she used to last year on the island. But Stephie's looking forward to starting from scratch, in a class where no one knows her or has preconceived notions about what she's like. A class where she can be Stephanie.

They leave the auditorium and go to their homerooms. The homeroom teacher for 1A is young, with short dark hair, and she's wearing culottes. She introduces herself as Hedvig Björk; she's going to be their math and biology teacher.

"Science, girls," she says. "Science is the future. I hope after four years with me that all of you will decide to continue on to a science program." She gives them a cunning look from behind her long, dark bangs. It's hard to tell whether she's joking or in earnest. Stephie likes Hedvig Björk already.

On the blackboard is a list of books they're supposed to have by tomorrow morning. Everyone copies down the titles, and Hedvig Björk explains that when they're finished in homeroom, anyone who wants to can go to the lunchroom and buy used books from the older girls.

There are thirty-five girls in the class. Tall, short, heavy, slim, with and without glasses. Most are more or less blond, but there are a few brunettes and one girl who looks as little like the fair Swedish girls as Stephie does. Stephie wonders what her name is and where she comes from. She decides to ask, but by the time she gets out of the classroom, the dark-haired girl is nowhere to be seen.

A group of girls gathers in the hallway around two blondes who are clearly friends. Although they're not sisters, they look very much alike, with big blue eyes and little round mouths. Their dresses are also similar, in the latest fashion, one green, the other blue. The girl in green is Harriet; the girl in blue, Lilian. They're the prettiest girls in the class, and they obviously know it.

Stephie goes to the lunchroom, where she finds a number of the textbooks she needs that aren't too dog-eared. She has to be economical with her scholarship money if she's going to make it last.

As she's leaving, someone calls her name.

"Stephanie, wait up!"

It can't be Sylvia or Ingrid; they would have called her Stephie. Puzzled, she turns around. Behind her is a round-faced girl with glasses.

"I'm May Karlsson," the girl says. "We're in the same class."

"I know," Stephie replies. "I saw you."

"Did you find any of the books you need?"

Stephie shows her the books she found.

"*German Grammar*, that's one of the most expensive," May says in an envious tone. "Lucky you! I only found these."

She shows Stephie a couple of books.

"You see," May says, taking Stephie by the arm, "I really have to scrimp and save. I have a scholarship to cover my books and my tram costs. If I didn't, my family wouldn't be able to afford to let me go to grammar school. I have six brothers and sisters, and my dad works in the shipyards."

"I'm on scholarship, too," says Stephie.

"Are you? I never would have guessed."

They go on talking as they head to the bookstore, where they buy the other books they need, as well as notebooks and school supplies. They're still chatting as they walk along the street. May goes into a bakery and buys a little bag of crumbled cookies. They sit on a bench and continue getting to know each other as they eat their broken treats.

"Do you want to sit next to each other at school?" May asks.

Stephie nods. "Yes, let's."

Then May gives Stephie her first tour of the city. She explains where the different tram lines go, and Stephie finally understands that although all the trams are pale blue, each one has a colored sign on the front with a number in the middle.

"See? The green line will take you to Mayhill, where I live, for instance," May says. "You have to go all the way out past the workers' community center to get there. But I guess there's no reason for you to come to our neighborhood. You live at such a fancy address."

"I'm nothing but a lodger," Stephie tells her. "I don't really live there."

Stephie tells May all about how she arrived on the island a year ago, and about going to school there, and how her teacher thought she should have a chance to continue her schooling. Aunt Märta and Uncle Evert refused at first, until the doctor's wife offered Stephie lodging with them and promised to help apply for her scholarship.

The church clock strikes twelve.

"I've got to be going. I look after my little brothers and sisters in the afternoons while my mother does domestic work," May says.

"Who's going to look after them when we have full days of school, then?" Stephie asks.

"We'll work it out," May says. "There are neighbors who can help. And Britten's eleven, so she can see to the younger ones some of the time. Here comes the green tram! See you tomorrow."

May boards the tram. Stephie finds her way back to the Söderbergs'. She spends the afternoon making paper covers to protect her books and writing a long letter home to Mamma and Papa.

She describes her new room, her school, and her home-room teacher. As always, she tries to be as positive as she can, not wanting to worry them. That's why she doesn't tell them she feels lonely in the big, empty apartment. Somehow she doesn't get around to telling them about May Karlsson, either.

six

The next morning when Stephie leaves for school, her bag is crammed full of books. Her lunch sandwiches are in the outside pocket. She doesn't have to bring her own milk; milk is served free of charge in the lunchroom.

Today Harriet and Lilian are wearing identical dresses with a floral pattern. Like yesterday, they form the core of a big crowd of giggling girls in the hallway. Stephie doesn't bother joining in. Not that she thinks they would make her feel unwanted, but she would probably just find herself standing on the edge of the group, not knowing what to say. Sometimes it's difficult for her to speak Swedish with people she doesn't know very well. She hasn't got all the nuances straight, and people sometimes misunderstand her.

May Karlsson arranges for them to be seated next to

each other in class. The dark-haired girl doesn't arrive until the last minute, sliding unobtrusively into a free seat.

Over the course of the day, they have five different teachers, but not Hedvig Björk, since they don't have math or biology on Tuesdays. They have old Miss Ahlberg, their Swedish teacher, a cute young sewing teacher, and a physical education teacher who lines them up in perfect rows on the schoolyard and who seems to love blowing her whistle: "One, two, jump, one, two . . . Keep those lines neat, girls!"

After gym comes the lunch break. When Stephie walks into the lunchroom, she sees the dark-haired girl sitting alone. Stephie gets her glass of milk and goes over to the table.

"Do you mind if I sit here?" she asks.

The girl nods uninterestedly.

Stephie didn't intend to be so straightforward, but the words just fly out: "You're Jewish, too, aren't you?"

"What business is that of yours?" the girl hisses. "Don't go getting any ideas. I'm Swedish."

Her angry reaction takes Stephie completely by surprise.

Had they been in Vienna, she would have understood it, supposing the girl was like Evi, who always said defensively, when the subject came up, that her mother was Catholic. But here in Sweden there's nothing wrong with being Jewish, is there? And if Stephie is wrong, if there is a different explanation for the girl's dark hair and brown eyes, all the girl has to do is say so.

"Sorry," Stephie mumbles. "I didn't mean any harm. . . . I was only wondering. . . ."

At that very moment May Karlsson comes over and sits down next to her. Oblivious to the tension, she starts joking with Stephie about the dictatorial style of the phys ed teacher.

"I bet she's going to make us do jumping jacks and calisthenics every time we have gym," May says. "She definitely doesn't seem like the kickball type."

The dark-haired girl gets up and walks off, leaving her glass of milk virtually untouched on the table. That's the only sign that she was even there. No waxed paper, no sandwich crumbs.

Their first teacher after lunch is Miss Fredriksson. They're going to have her for history and Christian studies.

"Anyone who wants an exemption from Christian studies has to have a certificate of affiliation with another denomination," she says.

In Vienna Stephie and the other Jewish children in the class had Judaism with a rabbi, while the Catholic and Protestant children had ministers from their own faiths. On the island it had never even occurred to anyone that Stephie might want to be exempted from Christianity. And in fact, she is Christian now. She has been baptized and accepted into the Pentecostal church.

She turns around and sneaks a look at the dark-haired girl, who is studying her cuticles with feigned indifference.

"Nobody?" Miss Fredriksson asks. Stephie feels like the teacher is staring straight at her.

"What about atheists?" May Karlsson asks. "Are we entitled to an exemption?"

"At your age," Miss Fredriksson replies, "you couldn't possibly comprehend atheism. I'll have no such nonsense here."

The last two hours of the day are German class. The girls are going to have German seven hours a week; lots of them are already complaining, even before the first class: "German verbs! And prepositions that take the accusative and dative!"

They've heard all about it from their older siblings and friends.

Stephie's got nothing to worry about. German is her native language, of course.

Their German teacher is Miss Krantz. With a z. Stephie hears the girls whispering about her, hears somebody call her the witch and the others hush her nervously. Miss Krantz is wearing a stiffly starched chalk-white blouse buttoned all the way to the chin. The heels of her shoes clatter hard against the floor as she paces back and forth in front of the class.

"Grammar is the foundation," she tells them. "If you don't master the grammar, you will never learn German properly, which means that you must be prepared to work hard. My classes require effort. In one semester I want you to be able to recite the prepositions that govern the accusative and the dative perfectly, in your sleep. If you haven't learned them, you will not receive a passing grade. Have I made myself perfectly clear?"

Stephie wonders for a moment whether Miss Krantz

really goes around waking her pupils up in the middle of the night, but decides she wasn't being literal. She isn't sure what the accusative and the dative are, but she'll figure it out, and nobody else seems to know what Miss Krantz is talking about, either.

Miss Krantz continues with a roll call, asking each girl to introduce herself by saying *"Ich heisse . . ."* followed by her name.

"Ich heisse Alice Martin," the dark-haired girl says.

"Ich heisse May Karlsson," May says, sounding more like she's speaking Swedish with a Göteborg accent than German.

"Ich heisse Stephanie Steiner."

Miss Krantz straightens up with a start.

"What kind of pronunciation was that? Where do you come from?"

"Aus Wien," Stephie whispers. From Vienna.

"Als Flüchtling?"

"Yes, I'm a refugee."

"Here we do not speak Viennese," Miss Krantz retorts. "At our school we speak proper German, as it is spoken in Berlin, capital of the Reich. And Fräulein Steiner will have to learn to do so as well."

Stephie feels her cheeks go hot. She never expected to be spoken to that way. Maybe German is going to be her hardest, not her easiest, subject after all.

"She's a horror," May whispers gently into her ear. "Don't let her get you down."

In the afternoon Stephie and Sven take Putte for a walk in the park across from the apartment. Stephie tells him about her teachers, and he tells her about his. Sven likes only one—the Swedish teacher who's encouraging him to write. All the others are old fogeys, in Sven's view, and there are even a few Nazi sympathizers.

"They shouldn't let people like that teach," Sven says. "But they think it's all right to be brown, as long as you're not red."

"Red?"

"You know, communist."

"Are you a communist?"

"No," Sven answers. "I guess not. But they've got a lot of things right. We need a society with much more equality. And all the old, rotten ideas ought to be done away with. Like inherited wealth. Military force. Public officials who only help their own kind."

Stephie puzzles. What he's saying sounds right, but still . . .

"The Nazis also want to do away with all the old ideas, and with the wealthy," she says. "And they're in favor of power for the people, too, or so they say."

"They're liars," says Sven. "The Nazis are on the payrolls of the big businessmen in Germany. The arms industrialists.

Then they go around blaming unemployment and poverty on the Jews."

Sven draws his hand through his hair until it stands on end. His brown bangs don't hang down as far over his eyes as when he came home from his hiking trip. One of the first things his mother insisted on was that he go to the barbershop.

"How long do you think it's going to last?" Stephie asks.

"What?"

"The war."

Sven sighs. "Hard to say. Things don't look very bright right now."

And they really don't. The Germans have occupied not only Denmark and Norway, but also France, Belgium, and the Netherlands. Italy has entered the war on the side of Germany, and just in the last few days, the Germans have begun dropping bombs over London. On the radio, the newscasters have reported a large number of casualties and injuries, with lots of people homeless, now that their houses have been bombed to rubble.

"What if they win?"

"The Germans?"

Stephie nods.

"Forget it," says Sven. "They don't have a chance. Don't you see?"

Stephie wishes she were able to believe him.

seven

$\mathcal{T}\textbf{he}$ boys' high school, where Sven is in his final year, looks like a citadel on a hilltop; it's a heavy redbrick building with little turrets at each end and a row of narrow slots up near the roof. In Stephie's history book there's a sketch of a medieval fortress with very similar turrets and slots, through which soldiers shot arrows to ward off their enemies. At her school, they sometimes sing a morning hymn about God being a mighty fortress, and it always makes Stephie think of Sven's school.

It's only a stone's throw from the dark citadel of the boys' high school to the sunny yellow school the girls attend. There's even a shortcut along narrow lanes leading between the lovely brick mansions above the lily pond and down through the park along graveled paths. Boys often stand outside the low wrought-iron fence by the girls' school when they finish for the day. Harriet and Lilian are the only girls in 1A who ever have boys waiting for them, though. Their "young men," two pimply fifteen-year-olds, are always there after school and sometimes even on lunch break.

Harriet and Lilian are the queen bees of the class. But they don't reign supreme by being mean, threatening, and bullying, like Sylvia did in Stephie's class on the island. Harriet and Lilian are always cheerful and nice to everyone. The others are attracted by their sweetness, like greedy flies to a sugar cube. Everyone wants to be friends with Harriet and Lilian, to bask in their glory.

Well, almost everyone. Not the bookworms, and not the most childish of the girls, the ones who still skip rope on the schoolyard. Not dark-haired Alice Martin, who keeps her snobbish distance from the whole class, and certainly not May Karlsson.

"Siamese cats." May snorts contemptuously. "They think about nothing but their appearance."

Sometimes Stephie stands at the edge of the crowd that gathers around Harriet and Lilian. She doesn't really want to be there, but at the same time she can't resist listening to the gossip about secret notes, promises, misunderstandings, and reconciliations.

"Love is divine," Harriet says with a sigh.

As if Harriet knew anything about love! A girl who keeps her admirer waiting, pretends to forget their dates, says she's going to let him kiss her and then changes her mind.

She teases him and annoys him intentionally, and Lilian does the same.

"You have to keep them hanging. If you don't, they get tired of you," says Lilian.

That's not love, and Stephie knows it.

She loves Sven.

She loves everything about him: his brown hair, the way it falls over his forehead, his gray eyes, and his high cheekbones. His voice, his hands, and the way he talks. And things you can't see. The essence of Sven.

She hasn't let on to him. She doesn't need to. For her, it's enough just to see him. For the moment, she wants to keep her love inside, like a warm little ball, a throbbing core she can touch gently now and then.

In due time, he'll understand. He'll be the one to reach out and touch her.

"Stephanie, I love you," he'll say.

She's no longer a little girl. Soon she'll have outgrown her rough undershirts and itchy woolen stockings. Then he'll see her as she really is.

Five years isn't a big age difference. Mamma is nine years younger than Papa. And Sven's even said he finds Stephie mature for her age.

"You almost seem older than some of the girls who are my age. Silly superficial girls who think about nothing but themselves. Promise me you'll never be like that!"

No, she is never going to be like those girls Sven despises. Or like Harriet and Lilian. She'll never hurt him, never flirt, and never be self-absorbed. She and Sven will mean everything to each other.

But not yet.

Stephie is sitting on one of the benches by the lily pond, thinking about all this and staring out across the gleaming surface of the water. It's the same bench she and Sven sat on that first evening. She sits here often, always on this very bench. Sometimes she's joined by a wrinkled old woman who feeds the ducks stale bread from a paper bag.

Stephie never brings anybody else here, not even May Karlsson. When she wants to go to the lily pond after school, she tells May she has to run an errand, and May walks down to the green tram's nearest stop, instead of keeping Stephie company partway down the avenue.

Two white swans are swimming in the pond, their heads held high. Swans live in lifelong "marriages." She learned that in Hedvig Björk's biology class. When the teacher said that, a giggle rippled from desk to desk, and someone asked whether swans fell in love just like people.

"Oh, you silly geese," Hedvig Björk admonished them. "Are your heads only full of one thing, girls?"

Now one of the swans extends his long neck and puts his head under his wing. He bobs on the surface, not moving. The dark green water-lily leaves are like little islands in the pond. The white flowers shine like stars, though the red ones at the far side are the prettiest sight of all.

Dark-haired Alice lives in one of the brick mansions

above the pond. Sometimes when Stephie is sitting on the bench, Alice passes by on her way home. May said that of all the fancy addresses in Göteborg, the streets above the lily pond are the fanciest of all, with their brick homes closed off from the rest of the city in splendid isolation behind stone walls. May also said that Alice's parents must be extremely wealthy.

May and Sven have one thing in common: they both think society is unfairly organized. But May believes that the Social Democratic Party is in the process of changing all that, and that the most important thing is for people like her, "ordinary people," as she says, to have the opportunity to get an education and become decision makers in society. She wants to be a politician herself.

"Then they'll see what May from Mayhill can do," she says, laughing.

"May from Mayhill" is an expression someone in the class started using one of the very first days of the semester. May wasn't offended, though her neighborhood is anything but hilly: she even calls herself that sometimes so no one can use the expression to make fun of her.

The sun disappears behind one of the tall trees on the other side of the pond. It's getting cold. Stephie heads for home.

She unlocks the front door with the key she has safety-pinned to the inside of her coat pocket. At first she was told to go to the kitchen door and ring the bell when she got home, but Elna got tired of her "eternal comings and goings" and asked Mrs. Söderberg to arrange for Stephie to have a key of her own.

"The girl has a good head on her shoulders," said Elna. "She won't lose your key."

Mrs. Söderberg ranted on at Stephie about everything that could happen if she lost it: the apartment could be broken into, the silver and the paintings could be stolen—"priceless works of art, you know"—the East Indian china might be broken, and the Persian rugs trampled with dirt.

Stephie finds Elna polishing the hall mirror.

"There's a letter for you," Elna says.

The letter is on the table under the mirror along with the rest of the day's mail. It's postmarked from Vienna, the first letter from home to reach Stephie in Göteborg.

The handwriting is Papa's.

My dear little Stephie!

We are so pleased you were able to go on to grammar school. You won't lose any time now that you're contin-uing your education just as you would have here if life had rolled along as we all imagined it would.

You wouldn't recognize anything here anymore. The war is a heavy burden on everyone, but of course it is worst for us Jews. The dwelling in which Mamma and I are living is already freezing cold, and I hardly dare to think about what it will be like when winter comes. Every morning Mamma has to walk the long distance to the home of the old woman she cleans and cooks for, while I walk to my work at the Jewish hospital. At the end of the working day, she has to walk for half an hour in the wrong direction to reach a shop where Jewish people are allowed to buy food. There are a grocery store and a dairy shop on the block where we live, but Jews may not shop there. You can imagine what a strain it is on Mamma. She is very thin now, and always tired. As I write, she is sleeping, which is why this letter will only be from me. Next time I'm sure you will hear from her, too.

Still, I do not mean only to complain about our conditions. The main thing is that you and Nellie are safe and have what you need. I do not think there is any risk that Sweden will be drawn into the war; you need not worry about that. And as I said, you have been able to continue your schooling. I'm sure you'll find the city environment more stimulating, too, than the isolation of the island. You'll be able to spend time with cultivated people and make friends of your own kind. . . .

Stephie puts the letter aside.

Cultivated people. Friends of your own kind.

What does Papa mean? Who are her own kind? Vera on the island obviously isn't. Stephie imagines that Papa wouldn't think May Karlsson is, either, not with her parents and six siblings all living in a one-bedroom apartment in Mayhill. Is dark-haired, nervous Alice Martin of Stephie's own kind? Are Harriet and Lilian? For the first time in her life, she has the upsetting feeling that her papa may not always be absolutely right, may not always know what is in her best interest.

eight

In early September Hedvig Björk takes the class on a biology excursion. Their other classes have been canceled, since they'll be gone all day. They take the tram and then have quite a long walk from the stop to Lake Delsjön. Their rucksacks are heavy with glass jars and bottles to collect aquatic animals and insects in. Hedvig Björk takes long strides at the head of the class.

The Söderbergs have lent Stephie a pair of Karin's old rubber boots; they're a little big and they flop as she walks along. She knows she looks silly with her too-big boots protruding from the nearly outgrown skirt she's wearing so as not to dirty her nice ones. She wishes she had a pair of trousers. Or a burgundy wool leisure suit with matching trousers and jacket, like Alice has.

The girls spread out along the lakeshore with their bottles and jars. Their prey is every living thing: worms and water spiders, beetles and leeches.

From a distance the water gleams blue in the sunshine, but standing at the edge, Stephie sees that it's brown and muddy, not clear like the seawater at the island. There is a scent of damp earth. The bottom is slushy and squishy underfoot. If you walk out too far, you sink in the sludge, and the water runs over the tops of and into your boots.

Hedvig Björk isn't the least bit bothered by wet feet. Her culottes are hiked up and she's wading around quite far out, more excited than any of her pupils.

"Look, girls," she shouts, "a whirligig beetle!"

Aquatic animals have peculiar names: diving beetles and backswimmers, marsh treaders and pond skaters. As if there were a whole little community down in the water, peopled by creatures, each with its own occupation.

A shimmering dragonfly lands on Stephie's arm, turning its round head and bobbing its little body. It's so lovely, with its transparent wings, that she'd rather let it fly away, but for Hedvig Björk's sake she turns a glass jar upside down over it, reverses the jar carefully making sure to place her free hand across the opening. Then she screws a top poked with holes over the dragonfly.

After a couple of hours, hot, dirty, and wet, the girls eat their packed lunches while sitting on a rocky ledge overlooking the lake. As usual, Alice keeps to herself. Stephie notices she doesn't have a single spot of dirt on her leisure suit.

"Alice," Hedvig Björk asks, "aren't you going to eat?"

Alice shakes her head. "I'm not hungry."

"Didn't you bring any sandwiches?"

"No."

"Have one of mine," Hedvig Björk says, offering her a cheese sandwich.

"No thank you."

"Do as I say, now," Hedvig Björk replies. "You need to eat if you're going to spend a whole day out of doors. Take it!"

Alice accepts the sandwich, taking tiny bites and eating extremely slowly.

After lunch break, Hedvig Björk inspects their bottles and jars. She admires Stephie's dragonfly.

"*Lestes sponsa*. A damselfly. And a fine specimen at that."

At first Stephie thinks she must be joking, but it appears the insect is really called a damselfly.

The afternoon is to be devoted to gathering plants for their herbaria. They are allowed to go one by one or two by two, as long as they don't get out of earshot of the whistle Hedvig Björk borrowed from the phys ed teacher, and can find their way back.

May isn't there—she's sick today—so Stephie heads off on her own. Alice walks away without so much as a glance at the other girls. Stephie goes in the same direction—not following on her heels, but more or less the same way. They are collecting ferns, mosses, and lichens. When spring comes, there will be flower excursions.

"Blue anemones, wood anemones, lilies of the valley! We'll go out into the woods once a week and watch spring develop," Hedvig Björk told them in class with great enthusiasm.

For a while Stephie keeps Alice in sight among the trees, but then she loses her. All she can hear is the cracking of twigs under her own rubber boots, the tweeting of the birds, and the wind murmuring softly in the treetops.

Stephie picks her plants carefully, folding them in pressing paper. When she gets home, she'll put them in new paper and lay them under a heavy pile of books. Some of the girls have real plant presses, but she wasn't able to afford one out of her scholarship money. When they're dry, each plant must be glued into a herbarium and tagged with its Swedish name, its Latin name, and the site where it was found.

Deep in the woods the moss is as thick and soft as an elegant carpet. The evergreen trees are dark and dense. Here and there are boulders, encrusted with moss and gray shield lichen. Stephie has never before been in a forest like this one. In the woods near Vienna, the wind whistles in the crowns of broad-leafed trees. On the island, what people called the woods was just stunted, windswept pine trees and bristly juniper bushes.

Suddenly something cranberry red appears among all the greens and grays. Alice is leaning into a bramble. At first Stephie thinks she must be picking a plant, but as she approaches, she realizes that Alice is bent forward throwing up. Stephie sees bits of Hedvig Björk's cheese sandwich in the moss.

"Alice," Stephie cries. "Are you all right?"

Alice looks up. "Go away," she says.

"Do you need something to drink? I've got some milk left."

"Get lost!" Alice yells. "Didn't you hear what I said?"

"There's no need to shout," says Stephie. "I was only trying to help!"

"I don't want any help," Alice retorts. "Especially not yours. Go away and don't you dare tell a soul about this."

Alice straightens up, brushing her hair back from her face. Her eyes gleam, black as pitch, against her pale skin. *She's so pretty,* Stephie thinks. *Haughty, pretty, and lonely.*

Stephie is seized by a sudden longing to be Alice's friend. Now they have something else in common, a shared secret.

"I promise . . . ," she begins, but Alice has already turned her back on Stephie and walked off in the other direction.

nine

Nowadays Sven has breakfast in the kitchen with Stephie. Elna makes them oatmeal and prepares Sven's lunch sandwiches. Stephie makes her own.

The doctor has coffee in the library before going to his office. His wife is almost always still in bed when Sven and Stephie leave for school. Sometimes, though, while they're eating, a loud bell rings and the number-five window on the panel by the door pops open. When that happens, Elna hurries to make up Mrs. Söderberg's breakfast tray.

The panel by the door is there to tell Elna what room the person is ringing from. Each room has its own button and its own number, which shows up in the kitchen when the bell rings. Stephie's room is number eight, but there is never any question of her ringing the bell. As Elna says, those bells are for the master and mistress. If Stephie wants Elna, she's supposed to go find her in the kitchen.

Stephie sees very little of Mrs. Söderberg and even less of the doctor. Some afternoons Mrs. Söderberg knocks on Stephie's bedroom door to ask if she's all right, and whether things are going well at school. But she never comes into the room; she stands in the doorway, as if she just happened to be passing.

About once a week Stephie is invited to the dining room for dinner. The rest of the time she eats in the kitchen with Elna. Sven thinks Stephie ought to be allowed to have dinner with the family all the time. He and his mother have quarreled about it.

Stephie doesn't really think it matters. Dinners with the doctor and his wife are stiff and formal and make Stephie feel bashful. When Sven's parents are around, she and Sven can't talk the way they usually do. She actually prefers sitting in the kitchen with Elna, at least on the days when Elna's in a good mood.

One afternoon Mrs. Söderberg knocks on Stephie's door. Stephie recognizes her knock, short and emphatic: *tap, tap, tap*. Elna knocks only once and then waits for a bit before knocking again, while Sven usually pounds out the rhythm of one of the swing melodies he plays in the evenings on the little portable Victrola in his room.

"Come in."

Mrs. Söderberg opens the door. "How is our little Stephie faring?" she asks.

"Fine, thank you."

"How is school?"

"Just fine."

That's usually the end of the conversation, but today Mrs. Söderberg doesn't leave.

"Incidentally, Stephie, we're having a dinner party on Saturday."

"Yes?" Stephie asks hesitantly. "I was thinking . . . I was planning to go home this weekend. I've been here for a month already."

"I expect that could wait," Mrs. Söderberg says, not even formulating her remark as a question. "We'd like so much for our friends to meet you, Stephie dear."

Stephie considers. She was really looking forward to going out to the island for the weekend. She's already phoned Aunt Märta to say she'll be coming, and her timing is good, since Uncle Evert is going to be spending both Saturday and Sunday in port. Fishermen can't let the days of the week govern their work.

Aunt Märta has surely told Nellie she'll be coming. And Vera's expecting her as well. . . .

But a real dinner party! She hasn't been to one in several years. A white tablecloth, folded napkins, candlelight, and floral centerpieces. Fine food, and wine gleaming in the grown-ups' glasses. Like in the old days, when Mamma and Papa had people to dinner.

"Yes," she hears herself say. "It can wait another week."

She phones Aunt Märta to say that she has to spend the

weekend in Göteborg. If Aunt Märta is disappointed, she doesn't let on.

The company is coming at seven o'clock, Elna tells Stephie. Early Saturday morning the cook arrives, and even before Stephie and Sven have left for their half-day of school, she and Elna are squabbling in the kitchen. Elna rushes out of the room, her face flushed.

When Stephie comes home, calm reigns in the kitchen. Elna asks her to help set the large mahogany table. They begin by inserting an extra leaf. Then they lay a soft felt protective cloth on the table and cover it with the shiny, ironed damask tablecloth, with its pattern of vines and bunches of grapes. Elna sets out two branched silver candleholders and a crystal vase that will later hold flowers on the table.

Stephie starts getting ready in good time. She puts on her flowery dress, the one Aunt Märta made for the final day of school last spring, and brushes her hair until it's shiny and smooth. She spits on her fingertips and curls her eyelashes, then pinches her cheeks to give them some color.

Mrs. Söderberg knocks while Stephie is standing in front of the mirror. She turns around, hoping for a compliment on her dress. Looking displeased, the doctor's wife raises her eyebrows and sighs.

"Don't you have a dark, solid-color dress?" she asks.

Clearly Stephie doesn't look right.

Mrs. Söderberg walks decisively over to the closet and searches through Stephie's clothes. That doesn't take long, and she obviously doesn't see the kind of dress she is hoping to find.

"Just a moment," she says, leaving the room.

She returns shortly with a dress on a hanger. It's a woolen one, so dark blue it looks almost black, long-sleeved and with a little white collar.

"This," she says, "will do, I think. Try it on!"

She stands just inside the doorway as Stephie wriggles her way out of her dress from the island and pulls the dark blue one over her head. Mrs. Söderberg helps her with the clasps at the neck and cuffs. Taking a step or two back, she surveys the results.

"Perfect!" she exclaims. "Elna has an apron for you in the kitchen."

"Apron?"

"Yes," says Mrs. Söderberg. "For serving. I did say, didn't I, that I want you to help serve the meal? Don't worry, it's not difficult. Elna will tell you exactly what to do."

Stephie's eyes burn with humiliation. She hasn't been invited to this dinner party as a guest; she's expected to be a serving girl in an itchy woolen dress that is much too heavy for this time of year. She feels like tearing the dress off and shutting herself in her room for the evening. But she doesn't. At six-thirty she's in the kitchen, where the cook has pointedly scattered dirty utensils for Elna to pick up and wash. Elna is muttering.

Stephie gets a little white apron to tie around her waist,

and Elna helps her pin a protective bib over the front of her dress. She's wearing the same getup herself, with a starched white embroidered band in her hair. Fortunately there isn't a second one for Stephie.

The guests arrive and are served sherry in the living room. Elna carries the glasses on a silver tray. When Mrs. Söderberg has clapped to get everyone's attention and has bid them all welcome, she tells them that dinner is served in the dining room. Now Stephie must collect the empty sherry glasses and carry them back to the kitchen. She tries to make herself as invisible as possible, and apparently no one notices her. Not even Sven, who's guiding an elderly woman by the elbow into the dining room.

Head bowed, Stephie serves the hors d'oeuvres, little sandwiches she offers from the right, as Elna has repeatedly instructed her: "Plates from the right, platters from the left!"

When she gets to Sven, she expects him to speak to her, but he continues his conversation with the elderly lady next to him, saying no more to Stephie than a simple "thank you."

Hors d'oeuvres, soup, main course, and dessert. Sherry, Madeira, red wine, and port. Gold-rimmed plates, silver cutlery, and crystal wineglasses.

Elna and Stephie do all the carrying in and out while the guests eat and chat.

"Yes, please, just a little more."

"No thank you, I've had quite enough."

As dessert is being served, Mrs. Söderberg claps everyone

to attention once more. Stephie is pouring liqueur into one of the ladies' glasses.

"The hostess doesn't normally give a speech," Mrs. Söderberg says, "but I would very much like to introduce someone. This is little Stephie, our lodger. She's the foster daughter of the fisherman's family we rented from last summer."

All eyes are suddenly on Stephie. She feels herself blushing. Although the glass she was pouring is full now, she can't seem to stop the thick liquid from running out of the bottle. The glass overflows, a sticky puddle forming on the tablecloth.

An instant later Elna has taken the bottle from Stephie's hand. Stephie escapes in the direction of the kitchen, hearing fragments of the conversation as she is leaving:

"Oh, the poor refugee child . . . She's not accustomed to this kind of dinner. . . ."

"No, from Vienna . . ."

"They couldn't afford to let her go on with her schooling. We're so pleased to be able to help. . . ."

In the kitchen she unties her apron furiously. Nothing Elna says can persuade her to go back into that dining room to offer seconds on the dessert.

ten

Late in the evening Stephie hears a knock on the door that separates her room from Sven's. By now Stephie has long since taken off the dark blue dress and gotten into bed in her nightgown, but she's not sleeping. She's sitting in bed with the light on, legs pulled up under her.

"Stephanie, are you asleep?"

Reluctantly, she answers. "No."

"May I come in?"

"No," she says again. "Leave me alone."

"Please, Stephanie, just for a few minutes. I have to talk to you."

"No."

"Stephanie! Don't be so obstinate. Just give me one minute."

"All right, then, if you insist."

Sven opens the door and closes it quietly behind him.

"I know you must be angry with me," he says. "You've got to understand, though, that there was nothing I could do. I've tried talking with my mother about her foolish decision for you to have your dinners in the kitchen—you know that. I didn't have the slightest idea she was planning for you to serve tonight. And in Karin's old funeral dress at that."

"You might at least have said hello," Stephie replies.

Sven is silent for a few minutes.

"You've got to understand, I'm dependent on them," he finally says. "Them and their accursed money. They support me and in return they expect certain behavior from me. Don't you see?"

"No!" Stephie shouts. "No, I don't see at all! Get out of here! Now!"

She lies down on her stomach, burying her face in the pillow.

◊ ◊ ◊

Stephie avoids Sven the whole week. She gets up earlier than usual, wolfs down her breakfast, and has already left the kitchen by the time Sven comes in. She spends the afternoons doing her homework in the school library or sitting on her bench by the lily pond. When she comes home, she sneaks quietly into her room and closes the door. On Saturday, a week after the dinner party, she's finally going out to the island. Straight from school she'll take the tram and then the ferry. She packed her bag on Friday evening and brought it with her. There isn't much in it but dirty laundry and a gift, a box of chalk she bought for Nellie.

When she walks out onto the schoolyard, she stops in surprise. Sven is straddling his bike on the other side of the fence, the brim of his school cap gleaming in the sun.

"Stephanie," he calls.

Harriet and Lilian, walking behind Stephie, crane to see who's calling her name. Stephie feels their curious gazes at her back as she walks to the gate.

"I thought I'd ride you to the ferry," says Sven. "Don't be angry anymore, Stephanie."

How can she be angry when he's looking her straight in the eye, his expression serious, but with the hint of a smile underneath it?

"I'm not angry," she says. "But we'd better hurry. The boat leaves in twenty minutes."

Sven puts her suitcase in his clamp and settles Stephie on the handlebars in front of him, his arms around her. Stephie can feel the eyes of every single person in the schoolyard glued to the scene.

"Bye, Stephie," shouts May. "See you Monday!"

The bike rolls smoothly away from the school across Götaplatsen and along the avenue, merging with the stream of traffic heading for the center of town. Stephie is so close to Sven she feels the warmth of his body on her back. Sven is whistling as he bikes, one of his swing tunes.

The ride to the pier is much too short. Sven slows to a stop and lets her off. He puts the kickstand down and carries her suitcase to the pier.

"See you tomorrow evening," he says. "Give my regards to the Janssons and say I hope they'll want us as tenants again next summer."

Stephie stands on deck until Sven is out of sight. Once they are out on the river, the wind feels colder. The leaves on the trees are beginning to turn yellow. It's fall, her second fall in Sweden. She goes into the passenger area, opens a book, and sits reading until they approach the island. Then she goes out on deck and looks eagerly to see whether anybody has come to meet her.

Everything looks as it always does: the breakwater, the pier, the little jetties, the fishing boats, the boathouses. Aunt Märta is waiting by one of them with her bicycle. Stephie gets off the boat when it docks and joins her.

"Evert hopes to be back tomorrow," Aunt Märta begins, "so you ought to get some time together."

Now, just like the first time Stephie arrived on the island, Aunt Märta gives her a ride on the back of her bicycle, and Stephie holds her suitcase on her lap. She wonders what Aunt Märta would say if she knew this was Stephie's second ride of the day on someone's bicycle.

The other on the bicycle of a boy, no less. A boy she loves.

It's not the kind of thing she'd ever talk to Aunt Märta about.

○ ○ ○

They stop at Auntie Alma's on their way home. Nellie runs outside, throwing her arms around Stephie.

"Why didn't you come last week?" she laments. "I've missed you."

Stephie rummages through her bag until she finds the wrapped box of chalk, and gives it to Nellie. It's a birthday present, her eighth birthday being just a few days off. Auntie Alma puts the gift away until then.

"I know Nellie. She won't be able to resist opening it otherwise," Auntie Alma says, smiling. They sit down to coffee for the grown-ups and berry juice for the children, and a while later Stephie and Aunt Märta continue their bike ride toward the white house on the west side of the island—the house at the end of the world, as Stephie called it when she first arrived.

Stephie takes a tour around the outside before going in. The dinghy is at the jetty, and the sheets hanging on the clothesline smell freshly laundered.

One of the first things Aunt Märta asks Stephie when they sit down to dinner is whether she has been to the Pentecostal church in Göteborg.

Stephie shakes her head.

"It wouldn't do you any harm to go now and then," Aunt Märta says dryly.

"We have so much homework," Stephie replies. "And if

I don't take my schoolwork seriously, my scholarship might not be renewed."

"Of course you must be attentive to your schoolwork. But your soul also has its needs," says Aunt Märta. "I worry about you. The city is full of temptations."

Stephie knows what Aunt Märta means when she uses the word "temptations": movie theaters and dance halls, lipstick and hair permanents. And boys.

"I study all the time," she repeats. "There's no time to even think about anything else."

"Fine," says Aunt Märta. "You're a good girl. You'll not let us down, I know."

Tonight Stephie goes up once more to the narrow bed in the room under the eaves. Her old teddy bear is waiting at the foot of the bed. His pitch-black eyes gleam lovingly in the dark.

eleven

Sunday mornings on the island used to mean Sunday school at the Pentecostal church. But now, when Stephie is there only to visit, she needn't go. Instead, she takes her bicycle and pedals off to Vera's.

Vera and her mother live in a little house at the far end of the huddle of homes around the harbor area. The house was once white but is now so dirty and abraded it looks gray. Some roof tiles are missing, and the door creaks loudly when Vera opens it to let Stephie in.

Vera's father drowned before she was born, a few weeks before he and Vera's mother were to be married. Vera is therefore an out-of-wedlock child, and when Aunt Märta says those words, she makes it sound like a terrible thing to be. Still, Aunt Märta likes Vera and doesn't object to her and Stephie's being friends.

Vera's mother pops her head out through the kitchen door to say hello. She's quite young—in fact, even younger than Stephie's own mother—but she looks weary and worn. Her hair, as red as Vera's, is disheveled, and she's missing two of her top front teeth.

"Come," Vera says, pulling Stephie up the steps to the attic. During the warmer months Vera has a room of her own in the unheated attic. In the winter she and her mother share a bedroom.

The attic is dark and musty-smelling. All kinds of indeterminable objects have been crammed in along the walls under the sloping roof; old blankets and rags hang over the rough ceiling beams. Stephie finds Vera's attic a little spooky; she wouldn't want to be up here on her own at night, and certainly not to sleep.

Vera opens the low door to her room and ushers Stephie in. It's big enough only for a bed and a box for Vera's clothes. She used to do her homework in the kitchen. This year, of course, Vera doesn't have any homework. She stopped school after sixth grade, like most of the other children on the island, and as Stephie would have had to do if it hadn't been for the doctor's wife and the scholarship.

She must try to remember that she's indebted to Mrs. Söderberg. She also owes a debt of gratitude to the people who award scholarships to "gifted girls of little means," as

65

well as to the Swedish relief committee, which made it possible for her to come to Sweden in the first place.

Aunt Märta and Uncle Evert are different. They don't expect her to be grateful to them for having taken her in, and for that very reason, she is extremely grateful.

◇ ◇ ◇

Vera and Stephie sit side by side on Vera's bed.

"What's it like," Vera asks, "in the city?"

Stephie describes the Söderbergs' big apartment while Vera listens, gaping.

"That's how I'm going to live when I grow up," she says.

Stephie has her dream of becoming a doctor. Vera's dream is to marry a wealthy man and live in the city, with loads of money, beautiful clothes, and housemaids.

When Stephie tells Vera about Alice, who lives in a huge brick mansion on the far side of the lily pond, Vera sighs deeply.

"Is the pond part of their yard?" she asks.

"No," Stephie tells her. "It's in a park."

"I want a mansion with a lily pond of my own in the yard," Vera says.

Stephie wishes she could tell Vera that wealthy, pretty Alice doesn't seem to be very happy, while May from May-hill is a cheerful girl, curious about everything. But she isn't able to find words that will make Vera understand.

"Good grief," she says instead. "What is a lily pond compared with having the whole sea outside your window?"

"Still, you don't miss being here, do you?" Vera asks. "Now that you have what you'd hoped for?"

"But I do. Sometimes. I miss Nellie. And you."

"Just as much as you miss being at home?"

Stephie answers after some consideration. Being at home would mean being with people she's known all her life, being able to speak her own language and not having to fear that people will misunderstand. Being at home means being in the place where she can be entirely herself.

"No," she says in the end. "Not just as much. Or, rather, not the same way."

"What about Sylvia?" Vera wonders. "Are you in the same class?"

"Nope. She and Ingrid are both in the other class. I never talk to them."

So Vera tells Stephie what she heard from Gunvor, who heard it from Majbritt, who heard it from Barbro: that a week ago, when Sylvia was home for the weekend, she had a note with her from her homeroom teacher, who wrote that Sylvia was going to have to work harder if she expected to pass.

Stephie nods. She's not surprised. At the island school Sylvia was considered a good pupil. She didn't have to put any effort into her schoolwork to get good grades. Things are different at the grammar school. Every pupil there was one of the best in her old class. And they all have to work hard to keep up.

"Serves her right," says Vera.

"Mmm," Stephie says, distracted. She can't really muster up any interest in Sylvia nowadays. To her, Sylvia is a person from the past.

They take a bike ride. It's a lovely autumn day. The air is clear and crisp. The heather has finished blooming, and the dwarf trees are beginning to yellow. They pick the last of the blackberries from their special bramble and ride along the road on which Vera once taught Stephie to bike. To Stephie, the island and Vera are inextricably linked.

◇　◇　◇

Auntie Alma brings her children and Nellie over to Aunt Märta's in the afternoon. Stephie notices that when she speaks German with Nellie, Nellie mixes in some Swedish.

"You mustn't forget your German," Stephie upbraids her. "It's really important. What will happen, otherwise, when we see Mamma and Papa again?"

"But there's no one for me to speak German with now that you've left," Nellie replies sulkily.

"Then read!" Stephie tells her. "Read your old books over again. And I'll give you mine, too. Write home at least once a week, as well. Promise!"

"I will," says Nellie. "But don't nag."

The grandfather clock on the wall is ticking. The boat back to Göteborg leaves at six o'clock. Stephie hopes Uncle Evert will get home before that. Otherwise another month will pass before she gets to see him.

Auntie Alma and the children leave at four-thirty. Aunt Märta sets three places at the kitchen table, but when the clock in the front room strikes five, Uncle Evert still hasn't arrived.

"I suppose we'd better eat," says Aunt Märta. "You mustn't miss your boat." By five-thirty they are finished with dinner and the dishes are done. Stephie's suitcase is packed with her clean sheets and underwear.

"We'd best be going," says Aunt Märta. "Nothing to be done about it."

Once again Stephie finds herself on the back of Aunt Märta's bicycle with her suitcase on her lap. At every turn of the road, she hopes to see Uncle Evert coming toward them.

"You'll see, he'll just have come into port and be down at the harbor," Aunt Märta assures her.

But when they get there, the berth where the *Diana* usually anchors is empty. Aunt Märta leans her bike against one of the boathouses and walks with Stephie onto the little pier where the steamboat picks up passengers.

Just as the steamboat is pulling out from the pier, Stephie hears a dull throbbing noise: a fishing vessel on its way in. It's the *Diana*.

Stephie rushes over to the other side of the deck. At the wheel of the *Diana* she sees Uncle Evert in his blue overalls and a heavy woolen sweater.

"Uncle Evert!"

"Stephie," he shouts, waving. "We had some engine trouble. Couldn't get here earlier."

"Never mind," Stephie calls back. "I'll be home soon again."

Home. Perhaps the island is home after all, but in a different way.

twelve

"Who is he?"

On Monday morning, the minute Stephie sets foot in the schoolyard, Harriet and Lilian pounce on her. Their eyes are bright with curiosity, their voices lowered to a secretive whisper.

"Who is he?" they ask again.

It takes a couple of seconds for Stephie to realize they're talking about Sven. Just long enough for Lilian to whisper, even more softly, "Gosh, he's so good-looking."

And Harriet: "Are you going steady? The two of you?"

"Are you? Don't keep us in the dark."

"Look, she's blushing! Come on, own up!"

"Yes," Stephie hears herself say, "we are."

The instant she utters those words, she regrets them. She

feels as if she has exposed her innermost self to public view. Not to mention that what she just said isn't true. She loves Sven, and she knows that when the time is right, he will love her back. But what there is between them now has nothing to do with what Harriet and Lilian call "going steady."

"Oooh!" Lilian sighs. "Aren't you the lucky one?"

"What's his name?" Harriet wants to know.

"Sven."

"Is he in high school?"

"Yes, he'll graduate this spring."

"When did you two meet?"

"Last summer," Stephie replies, thinking that if she keeps her answers short, they may tire of interrogating her.

"How?"

"He was a summer guest of my foster parents on the island."

"No, no," Harriet says impatiently. "I mean, how did you become a couple?"

Stephie knows she is on thin ice. She can't figure out an answer they'll believe. Instead of replying, she smiles as mysteriously as she can. "That's my secret."

"Oooh!" Lilian sighs again. "Please tell us."

"Some other time," says Stephie.

Stephie sees May making her way over to them. She definitely doesn't want May to hear what she just told Harriet and Lilian. May knows her much too well; she'd see right through her.

72

"Don't tell," she whispers to Harriet and Lilian. "May has no idea. You're the only ones who are in on it."

She feels terrible when she says that, being false and letting May down by keeping a secret with Harriet and Lilian. And a secret that's a lie, to boot.

"Sure," they say. "Our lips are sealed."

May doesn't ask her about Sven. Instead, she wants to know all about Stephie's weekend on the island. May was born in Göteborg and has lived here all her life, yet she's never seen the open sea. Stephie hopes Aunt Märta will let her invite May to join her on the island sometime.

Their first class on Monday mornings is German. By now Stephie, like all the others, knows very well what the accusative and the dative are. They've learned rhymes by heart to remind them which prepositions govern each and both.

"*An, auf, hinter, in, neben, über, unter, vor, und zwischen,*" they repeat in unison, Miss Krantz keeping time with her pointer against the edge of the desk.

What not a single one of them has done since the first day of school, however, is say a full sentence in German. They work on their grammar and read out loud from a boring textbook, translating the long sentences slowly and choppily into Swedish.

Stephie does her best to pronounce the words the way Miss Krantz does, but much too often she forgets and says them as she's accustomed to doing.

"Standard German!" Miss Krantz orders then, banging down the pointer. "In this class we speak standard German!"

73

After school, Stephie goes to the lily pond to be by herself and do some thinking. The weeping willows reflected in the water have begun to shed their leaves, and the ivy on the brick mansions is bright red. The water lilies are no longer in bloom, but the little islets of leaves still ornament the surface, and Mr. and Mrs. Swan are still floating there.

The bench feels cold against her thighs in the gap between where her underpants end and her stockings begin. She pulls her coat way down so she can sit on it.

All day Harriet and Lilian have been giving her conspiratorial looks, winking and smiling. They won't forget what she's said. It reminds her of when Putte gets a bone; they'll never let it go, not until they've squeezed every juicy tidbit out of her. She's going to have to tell them the things they want to hear.

Well, that won't be difficult. She's already pictured it all in her head, images of romantic scenes that will make Lilian sigh and Harriet long to hear more. Scenes she remembers from the magazines she and Evi used to read in secret at home, or from the movie posters pasted up outside the cinemas. Marvelous scenes starring her and Sven.

The hard thing will be not getting caught. She'll have to be extremely careful and keep herself on Harriet's and Lilian's good sides so they don't stop liking her and use her story as gossip for their mill. And most important of all, she must be sure May never catches on.

The worst part is that she feels like she's betraying Sven

by telling lies about him. If he ever finds out, she'll lose all her chances.

She's entangled in a net of her own making, as helpless as if she were caught in the clutching stalks of the lily pads and being pulled down toward the muddy bottom.

thirteen

My beloved Stephie,

I was thrilled to hear that you are happy in your new school. Your homeroom teacher really sounds like a wonderful person. It's important for a girl of your age to have an adult role model. I mean, a woman who is not her mother. You're growing up so fast, and even if we had not had to be separated, you would soon not be my little girl any longer. Of course, you will always be my little girl in one way. When things are hardest, I pull out the photos of you and Nellie when you were babies, and remember our wonderful days together.

Oh, I'm sounding morose, as if there were no future. But we must believe in the future. One day this nightmare will be over and we will be together again, all four of us.

The only thing that worries me is that since you are living in Göteborg now, you and Nellie will grow apart. You do visit her regularly, don't you? Nellie needs you. She's still such a little girl.

I'll have to stop now. We have no electric lighting and we have to be economical with the carbide for our lamp. Write soon and tell me everything that's going on! Please send my best greetings to all the kind people who are helping you, and remind Nellie to write to us.

Kisses from your mamma

Stephie sits on her bed, her mamma's letter in her hand. There is something peculiar about this letter, something ominous between the lines.

Although the words in the letter are loving and reassuring, Stephie is worried.

Her mother's handwriting has changed, too. It sprawls, as if her hand is no longer able to move the pen along the paper as gently and elegantly as it used to.

When Mamma and Papa told the girls they were sending them to Sweden, it upset Stephie, but she never doubted that it was the best thing to do. Back then they all believed that they would have to be apart for only a short time, that in a few months the whole family would have entry visas to the United States. "Six months at the very most," she remembers her father saying in a reassuring tone when she asked him how long it was going to be.

Now that Stephie knows they will probably not see each

other again until the war is over, she sometimes wonders if it might not have been better for her and Nellie to stay in Vienna. She knows that her parents are now living in a crowded dwelling, and that there is not enough to eat. She knows that Papa is hardly paid anything for the work he does at the Jewish hospital, and that Mamma is away from home from early morning until late in the evenings. She knows that they, like all the other Jews in Vienna, are living in constant fear of what the Germans will do next.

And yet she sometimes wishes she were there. She misses the scent of her mother and her soft cheeks, her father's warm hands and kind voice.

Even worse than missing them is feeling guilty. What right does she have to be sitting here well fed and content in a large brightly lit room on one of the finest streets in Göteborg when not only Mamma and Papa, but also Evi and other friends of hers, are freezing and starving? She ought to be in Vienna with them. She would be able to help Mamma clean houses. She would be able to make the long walk to the other side of the city to shop for food instead of Mamma, and to light the fire so it was warm when her parents came home in the evenings.

She would also, she knows, be another mouth to feed, and her parents would be sick with worry about her and Nellie if they were there. It's better for all of them that the girls are in Sweden, where the only signs of the war are that more and more products are being rationed and that cars run on smelly wood gas instead of gasoline. She knows this is true, yet it still seems unfair that she is here and they are there.

There's a knock on the door, to the rhythm of one of Sven's swing melodies.

"Come in."

Sven stands in the doorway, looking at her. "Am I disturbing you?"

"No."

He looks down at the letter in her hand. "From your parents?"

"Mamma."

"Any news?"

Stephie shakes her head. She can't explain the sense of dread that has come over her, not even to Sven.

"I really hope the Americans join the war," says Sven. "Then the Germans won't have a chance."

"Please, could you talk about something else?" Stephie asks hotly. "I'm tired of talking about the war."

Sven looks at her thoughtfully. Then he glances at his watch.

"Come on," he says. "You need cheering up."

"Where are we going?"

"You'll see."

As they put their coats on in the hall, Putte comes running, barking eagerly.

"Sorry, Putte pal," says Sven. "You've had your walk. This time you have to stay inside."

Stephie and Sven head toward Götaplatsen. Sven stops outside the concert hall.

"Here we are," he tells Stephie. "There's a concert starting in ten minutes."

Stephie feels pleasure warm her. It's been years since she listened to live music. Once the Nazis took over in Austria, Jews were prohibited from going to the cinema, the theater, and concerts. And on the island she isn't allowed even to listen to music on the radio. According to Aunt Märta's rules, and those of the Pentecostal church, music is sinful.

She feels a prick of guilt when she thinks of what Aunt Märta would say, but decides to ignore the feeling. Music has been part of her life since she was a little girl: her mother's piano playing and singing, her own piano lessons, the concerts and opera performances her parents used to take her to, especially the outdoor concerts in the Prater Park on summer evenings. There can't be anything wrong with that.

"What are you so deep in thought about?" Sven asks her.

"Nothing."

"Come on, then."

They find their seats at the back of the hall and settle in. The conductor raises his baton. The beautiful tones wash over her.

It's Mozart's Piano Concerto in D Minor. She remembers having heard it with Mamma and Papa ages back. That's the last thought she has before being completely swallowed up by the music.

The final notes echo and fade. Slowly Stephie comes back to the concert hall, to the applause from the audience, to Sven at her side. But she still feels completely at peace, and she has no desire to disrupt those feelings by talking.

"You're so quiet," Sven finally says when they're out on the square again. "Did you enjoy it?"

"Yes, of course," Stephie replies. "Thank you for taking me."

"Good," says Sven. "Now to the pastry shop."

They walk along the avenue and into one of the pastry shops, a lovely place with red plush seats and gold-framed mirrors.

"Have whatever you want," Sven tells her. "My treat."

Stephie picks a mille-feuille with shiny pink icing. Sven chooses the same and orders cocoa with whipped cream for her and coffee for himself.

They sit at a little round table. Stephie hasn't tasted anything this good in a very long time. She sips her cocoa slowly, trying to make the whipped cream last as long as possible.

"Sven," she says, "do you think it's wrong of me to enjoy myself like this when my parents don't even have enough to eat?"

"No," Sven replies. "You mustn't think like that. You're here because they want you to be well. They'd be pleased to know you were sitting here having a pastry. You mustn't let things that aren't your fault give you a guilty conscience. Do you understand?"

Stephie nods. When Sven says it, it seems perfectly clear that he is right.

fourteen

"*We* went to a concert on Saturday," Stephie tells Harriet and Lilian. "Afterward he took me to a pastry shop."

Although her words are true, she feels as if she's lying. Her big lie about Sven rubs off on everything she says about him. She feels uncomfortable about it. At the same time, it gives her a tingle of excitement.

Sometimes it almost feels as if the things she's telling them are true.

How they walk hand in hand when they're out with Putte. What he whispers in her ear when they're alone. How careful they have to be about keeping it all secret.

"His parents mustn't suspect anything," Stephie says. "And certainly not my foster parents. You know, my foster mother's Pentecostal. And terribly strict."

Harriet sighs. "You poor thing."

"You lucky thing," Lilian counters. "A secret love. It's so romantic."

"Has he kissed you?" Harriet asks. "For real, I mean, on the lips?"

Her question makes a warm wave wash over Stephie. She's been taken off guard.

"Not yet," she replies.

"Promise you'll tell when he does?" Lilian insists.

The whole next class, which is biology, Stephie imagines Sven kissing her. She shuts her eyes and fantasizes about his face coming closer and closer to hers until their lips touch. And then? She doesn't know. Her cheeks are hot and she feels almost sick to her stomach.

"Stephanie?" she hears Hedvig Björk say. "What's wrong? Are you unwell?"

Stephie opens her eyes at once.

"Yes . . . well, no." She hesitates.

"Do you need to go out for a breath of air?" Hedvig Björk asks solicitously.

"Thank you," says Stephie. "I'm all right, though, really."

She takes a deep breath and tries to concentrate on the large poster hanging in front of the blackboard. It illustrates different species of trees and their leaves; the girls are supposed to be copying the leaves into their notebooks.

May takes her aside between classes. "What's up with you today?" she asks in a much less concerned tone than

Hedvig Björk's. "You're acting so weird. What kind of secrets are you sharing with Harriet and Lilian?"

"None at all," Stephie says.

"Don't you think I have eyes?" May asks her coldly. "Or do you think I'm some kind of idiot? I see very well that you're always whispering together, and how you stop the minute I come along. I thought you and I were friends. Aren't we?"

Stephie is ashamed. May is like an open book. She never hides anything.

"Of course we're friends," Stephie assures her. "I didn't mean to hurt you."

◊   ◊   ◊

Stephie's doing well at school. She still makes spelling mistakes sometimes and puts words in the wrong order. But she reads in Swedish just fine now, and she has a very good memory.

Math is her best subject. Alice is the only girl in the class who can give her a run for her money there. When she or Alice goes up to the blackboard to solve an equation, Hedvig Björk always smiles.

"Look, girls, that's how it ought to be done," she says. "It's not really all that difficult."

When it's May's turn at the blackboard, Hedvig Björk always nods encouragingly to start with, but the more May mixes up her x's and y's, erases, and starts over, the more impatient Miss Björk grows.

"Oh, May," she finally says. "Can't you see what you're doing wrong? I can't understand how an intelligent girl like you can have so much trouble with algebra."

Stephie can't understand it, either. What makes this so difficult for May? As long as they're working just with numbers, she's fine. Square roots, compound interest, and other hard concepts aren't beyond her. But the minute there are both numbers and letters in the problems, May loses her grip.

Stephie offers to give May some extra help with her algebra. She thought they could sit in the school library, but May has a different idea.

"Let's go to my place," she says. "It's about time you came over."

Stephie remembers May telling her that her family lives in crowded conditions and that she has a whole brood of noisy little sisters and brothers. But she doesn't want to be rude and risk hurting May's feelings again. She's afraid May might think Stephie thinks her place isn't good enough.

"Sure," Stephie says. "It'll be fun to see where you live."

After school they take the green tram. It rattles slowly along, crossing the whole city center and then running beside a tree-lined canal. Stephie has never been in this part of town.

"There's the fish market," May says, pointing it out. "And the square with the workers' community center. See those buildings up on the hillside? That's Masthugget. We're getting close now."

The tram makes its way heavily up a long, steep hill, then down a gentler slope. May pulls the cord, and the tram comes to a stop.

Stephie looks around. There are no tall stone apartment buildings here, like in the neighborhood where she lives. All the buildings are three stories—the bottom one of stone, the next two of wood. The paint is flaking on the facades. The entryways open onto courtyards paved with cobblestones.

They turn into a cross street. The sign says CAPTAINS' ROAD, KAPTENSGATAN. After half a block, May turns in at an entryway, crossing the courtyard, where at least thirty children of different ages are playing. May points out her younger brothers and sisters.

"There's Britten. She's closest to me in age," she tells Stephie. "Kurre and Olle, the twins."

Kurre and Olle are two runny-nosed kids of about nine, as alike as two peas in a pod.

May lifts a chubby toddler and gives her a hug. "This is Ninni, our youngest. Got a kiss for May? Mmmm, what a nice kiss!"

May holds her little sister up proudly for Stephie to inspect. Stephie isn't eager to kiss Ninni. She's cute, but she also has a runny nose, and her face is dirty. Luckily Ninni decides to be shy, turning her head away.

"Britten," May calls. "She's soaked through! Aren't you supposed to be looking after her? And where are the others?"

87

Britten, a long-legged eleven-year-old in an outgrown dress, comes up to them.

"Gosh," she says. "I hadn't noticed. Can't you deal with her, since you're going upstairs anyway? It's almost my turn." She points to a group of girls jumping rope. "Erik and Gunnel went along with Mamma to work. Ninni's the only one at home. Please, can't you take her up with you?"

"I'll change her," May says. "But when that's done, I'll call you to come up and get her. Stephanie and I are going to do our math homework."

Britten looks at Stephie in admiration.

"Do you go to grammar school, too?"

"Yes."

"I hope I can go," Britten tells her.

"Britten," the girls with the jump rope shout. "Your turn!"

"She'll never get into grammar school," May tells Stephie once Britten is out of earshot. "She doesn't have good enough grades. She won't get a scholarship."

May carts Ninni up the stairs to the top floor. The door isn't locked, and it opens right into the kitchen, where there are a large table, four rib-backed chairs, a kitchen settle, a sink, and a shiny gas stove.

"Nice, isn't it?" May asks, striking the pale yellow enamel. "It's brand new. Until recently, all we had was a wood-burning stove."

With a deft movement she lays Ninni on the kitchen table. Holding her kicking little sister with one hand, she dampens a rag with the other. When she pulls Ninni's underpants down, the strong odor of urine fills the kitchen, and Stephie scrunches her nose.

"Why don't you go into the other room till I'm done?" May tells her.

Stephie goes into the only other room there is. It contains a sofa bed and two trundle beds, a little table, and a couple of chairs. She wonders how there is room for all of them to sleep there.

"Britten," May shouts through the open window. "Come and get her!"

Britten's rapid footsteps clatter on the stairs. When she has taken Ninni back outside, May comes into the other room, where Stephie's waiting.

"Which bed is yours?" Stephie asks.

"That one," May says, pointing to one of the trundle beds. "I share with Gunnel. Britten shares with Erik. Kurre and Olle sleep in the kitchen, and Ninni sleeps with Mamma and Papa on the sofa bed."

They sit down at the table and get out their math books and workbooks. In the beginning Stephie finds all the noise a distraction: loud voices from the courtyard, people running up and down the stairs, a radio blaring from somewhere, and a muffled ringing May says is noise from the workshop in the next yard. Soon, though, she's so absorbed by the algebra problems she doesn't hear a thing.

They have been at it for a couple of hours when the kitchen door opens. First two little kids rush in; then comes a heavyset woman wearing an overcoat with a housedress under it.

"This is Stephanie," May says.

"Tyra Karlsson." May's mother introduces herself as she extends a hand. "May has told us so much about you. It's a terrible thing to separate children from their parents. I wish I could flatten that Hitler between the rollers of the big mangle. We'd see how much harm he could do after a mangling!"

Stephie can't help laughing at the thought of Hitler rolled out as flat as a paper doll.

"And it's shameful how the government refuses to take in adult refugees," May's mother goes on. "As if there weren't room for a few more people in Sweden. If nine people can live in this apartment, I imagine there are others who could shove over."

May's mother asks whether Stephie will be staying for dinner, but Stephie has promised Elna she will let her know in advance if she won't be home to eat.

"Well, you'll stay next time, then," May's mother concludes. "I want you to know you'll always be welcome here."

◇　◇　◇

May walks her to the tram stop. Walking down Kaptensgatan, Stephie notices a young man coming out of a tavern. He looks like . . . Oh, it really is Sven! He's walking rapidly toward the tram stop, about twenty yards ahead of her and May. What is he doing here?

As they pass the tavern, Stephie peers in through the window. It's an old-fashioned workingmen's tavern, dimly lit, with scruffy brown furniture and beer glasses on the tables. A few of the tables are occupied by men, all sitting alone and dressed in worn-looking clothes. A young girl is wiping one of the messy tables with a dishcloth. She's bent forward over the table, her hair falling in front of her face, but just as Stephie passes, she looks up to answer a question from one of the men.

Stephie sees Sven at the stop from a distance. Before Stephie and May can get there, a tram pulls up. Sven gets into the front car.

"Run. You can make it," May says.

Stephie picks up speed and manages to get through the back doors of the car just as they're shutting. She pays the conductor for her ticket.

At Valand, the stop closest to the Söderbergs' apartment, she sees Sven get off. He turns onto the street that leads home. She continues to another stop and walks from there, not wanting Sven to know she saw him.

Not until she has figured out what he was doing at a tavern in Mayhill.

fifteen

The second time Stephie goes home to the island for the weekend, the autumn storms have started. The evening before she leaves, the wind howls outside her window and the rain hammers against the glass. In the morning she can see that huge branches have blown off the trees in the park. The almost leafless treetops along the street are flapping, and the clouds are racing across the sky. The sidewalk is slippery with wet leaves.

Stephie has a book to read, and as long as the boat is on the river, she sits in the passenger area, engrossed. That changes the instant the boat hits the open sea, and the waves bang wildly at the sides of the boat. Stephie drops her book. Nothing seems to be staying in place; everything is rocking and reeling. Suitcases and baskets slide along the floor, from one side to the other, and back again. A baby begins to wail.

The stagnant air is overpowering. The scents of coal smoke, damp woolen garments, and perspiration make Stephie nauseous.

The little baby throws up in its mother's lap. For Stephie that smell is the last straw. Dizzy and sick to her stomach, she rushes out on deck.

Over a year ago, when Stephie first went to the island on the boat, she was seasick, even though the wind wasn't blowing nearly as hard then as it is today. She's never dared to tell anyone, but last summer when Uncle Evert wanted to take her along on a fishing expedition on the *Diana*, she said no.

The boat trip out to the island takes only a couple of hours. *We're almost there*, she tells herself, but soon she has to lean over the rail and vomit. When her stomach is empty, she leans her head back, letting the rain rinse the cold sweat from her brow.

When the boat finally pulls up along the pier on the island, Stephie is exhausted and soaked through. Her knees feel like jelly and her head is spinning. She has to hold tight to the railing as she walks down the gangway.

"Stephie?"

It's Uncle Evert's voice. Looking around the pier and boathouses, Stephie doesn't see him.

"Stephie, over here!"

His voice is coming from one of the little jetties. Uncle

Evert is standing by the dinghy. Weak-legged, she makes her way over to him.

"I came by boat," he says. "It's such terrible weather for you and Märta to have to bike in."

Stephie's forgotten the rain that was whipping at her face. All she knows is that she's still feeling seasick. The very thought of getting into another boat, even to travel the short way around to the other side of the island, makes her feel ready to throw up again.

"Goodness, you look terrible," Uncle Evert goes on. "Like a drowned cat. Did you spend the whole trip on deck?"

Stephie nods faintly. "I was seasick," she whispers.

"Good gracious!" Uncle Evert replies. "How shall we get you home? Can you manage a second boat ride?"

"I'm not sure."

"We'll give it a try. You need to get indoors and change to dry clothes if you don't want to end up in bed with pneumonia."

Uncle Evert takes her hand, supporting her as she gets into the boat. He helps her off with her wet coat and pulls a big woolen sweater over her head. It's an extra he had stowed away under the front bench. Then he helps her into a slicker that hangs way below her knees. After that, Uncle Evert spreads another slicker along the wooden plank bottom and rolls a scarf up for a pillow.

"You lie there," he says. "And focus on the horizon the whole time. That helps."

He starts the motor and pulls out from the jetty.

The rain rinses her face again. Even though the little rowboat rides the waves heavily, her seasickness does not get worse. She's not even cold. Instead, she feels as if her body is going numb. Fatigue engulfs her. She closes her eyes.

When she wakes up, she's in her bed in the little room under the eaves. Someone has removed her shoes and the slicker, but she's still wearing the heavy sweater. It smells of fish, oil, and Uncle Evert. It's nearly dark outside. She must have been asleep for some time.

Cautiously, she tries to sit up. She's no longer dizzy. Actually, she's ravenous.

In the kitchen, Aunt Märta is preparing dinner.

"I surely didn't expect you to come home like that!" Aunt Märta says by way of a greeting. "When Evert came in with you in his arms, I was sure there had been an accident. You'd better change your clothes now. I imagine you're damp through and through."

"May I please have a glass of milk first?"

Aunt Märta nods. "Would you like me to heat it up?"

The milk smells sweet and mild. Stephie sniffs at the steam rising from the cup before she takes a sip. The smooth warmth spreads from her stomach to her whole body.

Aunt Märta has lit the wood-burning stove. The heat in the kitchen fogs up the windows. The sound of the rain outside combines with the crackling of the burning wood and the soft scrape of Aunt Märta's peeling potatoes for dinner.

Soon they'll be sitting at the table: Stephie, Aunt Märta, and Uncle Evert. Like a family.

She spends Sunday morning with Vera. In the afternoon she and Aunt Märta and Uncle Evert go to Auntie Alma's. Since the *Diana* is not out fishing, Auntie Alma's husband, Uncle Sigurd, is also at home. While the grown-ups sit around the table, Stephie goes up to Nellie's room with her.

"Stephie?" Nellie asks. "Do you think God loves Mamma and Papa?"

"Of course he does," says Stephie. "Why wouldn't he?"

She has to bite her tongue to resist adding, "If there is a God, of course."

May doesn't believe in God. Stephie isn't sure about him herself. But she doesn't say anything about it to Nellie.

"Well, because Mamma and Papa don't believe in Jesus," Nellie says. "I was thinking that was why God isn't looking after them. Because they—what are the words?—have denied God's only begotten son?"

"Who's been putting ideas like that into your head?" asks Stephie. She knows Nellie could never have come up with anything like that herself.

"The new parson." Nellie frowns. "He says the Jews murdered Jesus and that God is angry with them for it. Stephie, are we still Jews even though we've been redeemed?" Her big brown eyes are glassy, and her bottom lip is trembling.

"Yes," Stephie tells her. "We are Jews. And it's nothing for you to be ashamed of. We didn't murder Jesus. You didn't,

I didn't, and Mamma and Papa didn't. Nobody we know did. That all happened two thousand years ago. And it's nothing to blame people who are alive today for. One thousand years ago the Swedes were Vikings who pillaged and murdered wherever they went. Imagine trying to blame the Swedish people who are alive today for what the Vikings did. See what I mean? You mustn't believe what the new parson has been telling you."

"Are you sure?"

"Absolutely."

"On your honor?"

Stephie looks Nellie right in the eye and says, "Honest to goodness." Nellie looks relieved.

"Stephie?"

"Mmm?"

"I don't like you living in Göteborg. I wish you still lived here."

"But I can't go to school here."

Nellie thinks about that. "Couldn't I move into the city with you, then?"

"You wouldn't be happy there," Stephie tells her. "You'd miss Auntie Alma and the little ones and your classmates. You're much better off here."

"I want us all to be together," Nellie says. "You and me and Auntie Alma and Uncle Sigurd and Elsa and John and Sonja and everybody in my class except Mats, because he's such a nuisance. And Aunt Märta and Uncle Evert and the family you're living with now and Vera and May or whatever her name is. And Mamma and Papa. I miss Mamma and Papa. I'm going to pray to God to arrange for them to come here."

"Yes, do," Stephie says, although she doesn't really think God has much say in the matter. "Do that, Nellie."

sixteen

Autumn spreads over Göteborg like a wet gray blanket. The humidity rises off the river and the canals, and although it's still above freezing, the winds are icy cold.

Darkness in the city is different from darkness on the island. It's not black; it's gray, lessened by all the city lights: streetlights and neon signs, the sharp glare from the street-level shop windows, and the gentler glow from the apartments upstairs. It never gets truly dark, but it's never really light, either; dusk falls almost imperceptibly in the late afternoon.

The winter coat Stephie's parents gave her before she left Vienna is getting snug. Her wrists are cold; she has to pull down the sleeves of her sweater to cover them. She wishes she could get a pair of gloves with long cuffs, like most of the girls in the class have. She's embarrassed about wearing the mittens Aunt Märta knitted. But she's going to have to wear them soon, even on the schoolyard. Her hands are getting chapped and red from the cold.

Since the first time Stephie went to May's after school, she has been going home with her once or twice a week. She helps May with her algebra, and May helps her with her Swedish. Sometimes she stays for dinner with May's noisy, lively family. May's father is very funny; his jokes make the children double up with laughter.

Every time Stephie walks between May's door and the tram stop at Kaptensgatan, she's on the lookout for Sven. Once, she thinks she sees him walking into the tavern, but she's far away and knows she might be mistaking someone else for him.

◊　◊　◊

One day in early November, Harriet and Lilian take her aside on the schoolyard.

"Has he kissed you yet?" Lilian asks.

"Nope."

"Strange," Harriet says, "considering he's almost grown up."

"He's holding back for my sake," Stephie lies. "Because I'm so young. He doesn't want to do anything that might get me in trouble."

"Oooh, how romantic," Lilian replies. "Like in a movie."

"Speaking of movies," Harriet says, "they say the one that's showing at the Lorensberg is really good."

"What's it called?" Stephie asks, mainly to change the subject.

"'*Til We Meet Again*," Harriet says. "A love story. But they let you in even if you're under fifteen."

"Want to go?" Lilian asks eagerly. "All three of us?"

"Sure," says Harriet. "How about Saturday?"

Stephie hesitates. She knows that to Aunt Märta, going to the movies is worse than going to a concert. On the other hand, how would Aunt Märta ever find out if, just this once, she went to the movies in Göteborg?

"How much is it?" she asks.

"Ninety-two öre for the cheapest seats," Harriet tells her.

Stephie has only fifty öre in her piggy bank. She'll have to borrow another fifty and repay it from the allowance Mrs. Söderberg gives her every Sunday. But who can she borrow from? May never has any money, and anyway, Stephie wouldn't want May to know she was going to the movies with Harriet and Lilian.

◊   ◊   ◊

"Could I borrow fifty öre?" Stephie asks Sven.

"Sure. What are you going to buy?"

It would be easy to lie and say a book. But Sven would want to know what book, and he might ask her how it was later. She decides to tell it like it is.

"I'm going to the movies," she says. "With two of my classmates."

"What are you going to see?" Sven asks. "*The Grapes of Wrath*? It's supposed to be really good. I'm going to see it."

Stephie wishes that were the film she was going to.

"No," she says. "'*Til We Meet Again*."

"Oh, a romance," Sven says in a teasing voice. "What could you know about love? You're only thirteen!"

"I might know more than you think."

"Ah," Sven replies. "Who's the lucky fellow?"

Wishing she hadn't said anything, she doesn't answer. If only she hadn't told him the name of the film. And if only she hadn't asked Sven to lend her the money.

"Some film star, I bet," Sven continues. "Let me guess! Cary Grant? Leslie Howard? Maybe Clark Gable?"

"Cut it out!" Stephie says, ready to burst into tears. What on earth does he think of her?

"I was only joking," Sven tells her. "Don't get upset."

◊   ◊   ◊

When Saturday evening comes around, she combs her hair extra well and puts on her best dress, even though she knows no one will see it under her coat. They're meeting outside the movie theater at a quarter to seven. It's not far away, only on the other side of the main avenue.

She arrives in good time. There's already a long line outside the door. The building is brightly lit and reminds her of a Greek temple, with fluted columns on the facade. Stephie gets in line, and soon Lilian arrives, followed shortly by Harriet.

They buy their tickets and a bag of toffees to share. An usher in a uniform takes their tickets.

"Well, girls, I hope you have your handkerchiefs ready," he says, smiling. "This one's a real tearjerker."

First come the newsreels, beginning with one about a bicycle race for delivery boys. The winner is Lasse, a freckle-faced young man with a crooked front tooth that stands out when he smiles and waves at the camera.

Then there's a German newsreel from the war, showing an airfield near the English Channel and aircraft being loaded with bombs. When the planes take off, the camera follows them. The German planes search out an English fighter plane and shoot it down. In flames, the English plane nose-dives to the ground.

Stephie wonders if the pilot had time to parachute out. The cheery voice of the speaker doesn't mention him.

The curtain closes and then opens again slowly to music, and the feature film begins.

A man who was condemned to death in San Francisco has escaped but is caught by a detective in Hong Kong. On board the ship that is to transport him back to be executed, he meets a beautiful woman, pale and dark-haired. She's suffering from a fatal heart disease and doesn't have long to live. They fall in love but don't dare to reveal to each other that their days are numbered. When they embrace for the last time, they both know they will never meet again, but each is trying so hard to spare the other's feelings that they don't speak of it.

It's a sad and beautiful story. Stephie's tears run down her cheeks, and she hears Lilian sniffle loudly.

In a daze, they walk out through the side door along with the rest of the audience.

"I thought it was just wonderful," says Lilian. "And she was so gorgeous in that long gown."

"Dark hair is so attractive," Harriet says. "You're lucky, Stephanie. Brunettes are definitely more mysterious than blondes. More romantic, too."

"She reminded me of Alice," Stephie says.

"Alice Martin? Not in the least!" Harriet sounds indignant. "Alice's face is a whole different shape. If the actress looked like anyone, it was you."

"You're joking," says Stephie.

"I am not," insists Harriet. "You've got big eyes like hers, and long eyelashes."

They're so busy talking they don't notice the people around them. By the time Stephie spots a familiar face in the crowd, it's too late to get away.

It's the round, cheerful face of Miss Holm, the lady from the post office on the island, and the gossip monger of the community.

"Well, if it isn't our little Stephie," she says. "So you were at the movies, too? Imagine! I thought the Janssons were religious. This is my sister, who lives here in Göteborg. And

I suppose these girls are your classmates. How nice to see you, dear. Drop in to the post office the next time you're visiting, and we can have a chat."

Stephie is rigid with fear. On Monday Miss Holm will be behind the window at the post office, telling every single customer about her visit with her sister in Göteborg, about how they went to the movies, and how she happened to see Stephie outside afterward. By Tuesday, at the very latest, Aunt Märta will know all about it, as will all the other members of the Pentecostal church.

seventeen

The whole week after the movies, Stephie keeps expecting Aunt Märta to turn up at the kitchen entrance in her city coat and hat, to give Stephie a good talking-to or even to take her back to the island, away from the temptations of city life.

But Aunt Märta never appears. Could Stephie have been lucky? Could Miss Holm have forgotten all about it? Perhaps she didn't find it so remarkable to bump into Stephie in Göteborg. She probably had lots of other interesting things to tell people after her visit.

On Thursday after school, Stephie goes to May's. As they're walking from the tram, she sees Sven in front of them on the street. This time there is no doubt about it: he's no more than twenty yards ahead and Stephie knows it really is him. He turns in at the tavern. Stephie slows down enough to have a look through the window. She watches Sven hang up his coat and sit down at a table. His back is to the window and his body is blocking the table, so Stephie can't tell if there is anyone sitting opposite him.

"What are you looking at?" May asks. "Was that somebody you know?"

"No," Stephie says. "I got it wrong."

"That makes sense," says May. "I didn't think you knew anybody around here."

The minute they walk into May's courtyard, Britten comes running.

"May, May," she shouts. "Hurry up! Ninni can't breathe."

May rushes over with Stephie at her heels. Ninni's sitting in the pile of gravel that serves as a sandbox, coughing and gasping for air, trying to scream. Her little face is going blue and she looks as if she is choking.

"Ninni," May screams, picking her up in her arms. "Ninni, don't die on us!"

Suddenly Stephie remembers something from a very long time ago, when Nellie was little.

"Quick, we have to get her inside," she instructs May. "Britten, do you know where your mamma is?"

Britten nods.

"Run as fast as you can. Tell her she has to get hold of a doctor. Ninni has the croup."

"How do you know?" Britten asks.

May just gives her a push. "Didn't you hear what Stephanie said?" she shouts. "Go on!"

Britten rushes off while May runs up the stairs with Ninni in her arms and Stephie right behind.

"We have to boil some water," Stephie tells May.

May nods. "Take the big enameled pot from the larder."

Stephie lights the gas stove and fills the pot with water. Ninni has a hacking cough. It sounds awful, as if something inside her were smashing to pieces.

"Are there some old sheets we can soak and hang up?" Stephie asks.

"Take the twins' sheets from under the settle."

Stephie pulls out a set of sheets from beneath the kitchen settle and holds them under the faucet. Once they're soaked, she hangs them over the kitchen washing line. Dripping water makes a puddle on the floor.

Ninni's whole body is arched, and she's gasping for air. Her little round face is blue and pale.

"Do you have an umbrella?"

"An umbrella?" asks May in bewilderment.

"She has to inhale steam," Stephie explains. "We need an umbrella to keep the steam close to her."

"No, we don't have an umbrella," May says, almost beside herself with fright. "She's dying, can't you see she's dying?"

"We'll use a blanket instead," says Stephie.

She pulls a blanket out of the drawer under the settle. May is sitting on a chair, rocking Ninni in her arms and weeping.

Finally the water begins to boil.

"Come over here," says Stephie. "Hold her as close to the pot as you can without getting scorched."

May places Ninni's head over the steaming pot. Stephie takes the blanket and makes a tent of it over Ninni, May, and the boiling water.

After just a few minutes, Ninni is coughing less and breathing more easily. At first she struggles as if to free herself from May's grip, but a few minutes later she has calmed down and relaxed.

"I can hardly breathe in this heat," May says from under the blanket. She pops her head out, her face all red and her glasses fogged up.

"Want me to hold her for a while?"

They change places.

Under the blanket the heat is unbearable. Ninni's little body is sweaty and slippery. Stephie feels a surge of relief when May's mother comes rushing in with Britten close behind.

"I've got a taxi outside. Give me Ninni and I'll take her to the hospital."

They carry Ninni down to the taxi and make another little tent in the backseat out of one wet sheet covered by the blanket. May's mother shuts the door and the taxi takes off.

"How did you know what to do?" asks May.

"My papa's a doctor," Stephie says. "That's what he did when my little sister got the croup."

After a couple of hours, May's mother is back. Ninni has to spend the night in the hospital.

"But she's out of danger," May's mother tells them. "The attack passed, and when I left, she was asleep. The doctor said it was lucky she got to inhale steam right away. Things could have been much worse otherwise."

"I was so scared," says May. "I thought she was dying."

"You both did an excellent job," May's mother says. "Stephanie, you must know how grateful I am."

Grateful. For almost a year and a half, Stephie has heard people telling her how grateful she ought to be to everyone who has helped her. Now May's mother is grateful to her. It's an unexpected pleasure.

May's mother doesn't go back to work. She sits in the kitchen over a cup of coffee for a long time.

"After an experience like this, we deserve a little treat," she says, sending Britten to buy two Danish pastries. Stephie and May get to split one; May's mother shares the other one with Britten.

No homework gets done that afternoon. The other women in the building heard the commotion and saw the taxi, and they drop by, one by one, to find out what the excitement was all about. May's mother pours them coffee and tells the story over and over again. The women share their woes and compliment Stephie and May for saving Ninni.

Stephie finds all the attention a little embarrassing, but at the same time, she's proud of herself. As she walks to the tram, her head is so full of the afternoon's events she doesn't even remember to be on the lookout for Sven.

eighteen

Wh̄en she gets home that evening, there's a letter on the table in the hall.

Dearest Stephie,

Thank you for the letter. It gave us great pleasure. And please forgive our delay in answering! We're working so hard and have such long days, it's difficult to make time for the most important thing of all: writing to you and Nellie. Mamma had to stop working for the old woman. She works at a factory now, which means she has even farther to walk than before. In the evenings she spends hours standing in line at the special stores where Jews are permitted to shop, where all they sell is rotting vegetables and meat that has gone bad from the regular shops. As for me, I continue to walk back and forth to the Jewish hospital, as Jews are no longer allowed

111

on tram number 40! Life has become more and more unbearable, and everyone who has a way is trying to get out of Vienna. Your friend Evi and her parents left last week. For a very long time they felt safe, what with Evi's mother being Catholic, but the persecution is now so pervasive that no one escapes. They have gone to live with their relatives in Brazil, traveling via Portugal. We've filed another application with the United States consulate, along with your aunt Emilie and her husband. Aunt Emilie has managed to make contact with a distant relation in New Jersey, who has promised to try to help us. Maybe we will have better luck this time. In any case, we have not given up hope and will not as long as we know our girls are there waiting for us. But if we fail, and if we are not able to write very often, you must know that we are thinking of you and Nellie, that we think of you every day, even every hour.

With much love from your papa

In an instant all the pleasure she was just feeling is swept away.

Imagine if she had been able to come home and tell her parents what she had done that day! They would have been proud of her, she knows.

Why should she be the one with a dark shadow hanging over her all the time?

Why can't she be like the other girls, who worry most about getting a bad grade, or having a nose that's too big?

Why did her parents send her away?

For her own good, she knows, but still . . .

She feels lonely, terribly lonely and abandoned.

She hears a melody coming from the other side of the wall.

Warily, she knocks on Sven's door.

"Come in."

She opens the door.

"Oh, it's you. Come in and sit down."

Sven lifts a pile of books and papers off a chair and sits down on his bed. Stephie just stands in the middle of the room.

"What's wrong?" Sven asks. "What's happened?"

That's when she begins to weep. Not sobbing, just tears running silently down her cheeks.

"Stephanie," says Sven. "Poor you. Come here and sit down."

When she still doesn't move, he gets up, takes her by the hand, and leads her over to the bed. Sitting down next to her, he puts an arm around her shoulders. She leans her head on his chest, feeling his warmth. He smells faintly of aftershave. She has never been this close to him before.

They sit perfectly still. She wishes that this moment would last forever, that they would never move—Sven with his arm around her, her with her head to his chest. She can hear the beating of his heart.

In the end, he's the one who shifts. Turning to the side, he puts one hand under her chin and raises her face to his.

Now, she thinks, shutting her eyes. *Now he'll kiss me.*

She parts her lips slightly, like the film stars do.

But Sven doesn't kiss her. Opening her eyes, she sees him take a clean handkerchief out of his pocket and wipe away her tears. Then he releases her, gets up, and walks over to the Victrola. Only now does Stephie realize that the music has ended and that the needle has been scraping the middle of the record.

"Tell me, what happened?" He pulls the desk chair over so he's sitting opposite her.

"There was a letter from Papa," she says.

"What was in it?"

"It's so awful. Mamma has to work in a factory now. They have hardly anything proper to eat. Papa is no longer permitted to take the tram to work. And Evi's left for Brazil. I may never see her again."

It's as if the dam has burst. Everything Stephie's been keeping pent up inside spills out: all her thoughts and her dreams, all her longing and her worries.

Sven listens.

"I wish I could help you," he says when she finally stops. "That I could do something so your parents would be able to come here."

Stephie nods without saying anything. She knows there is no more to be done. Aunt Märta and Uncle Evert, and even Mrs. Söderberg, have already done all they can to help Mamma and Papa get entry visas for Sweden.

"Friends have to be able to talk to each other about everything, don't they?" Sven asks her then.

Stephie nods again. But she can't help wondering whether Sven really talks to her about everything—or whether he's keeping certain things secret. Things having to do with Mayhill and a tavern.

nineteen

$\mathscr{A}$ week has passed since Stephie was at the movies, and no punishment has yet been called down on her, by God or by Aunt Märta. Still, she's worried about what will happen the next time she goes to the island.

The fall semester is drawing to a close, and schoolwork is taking more and more of Stephie's time. There are several quizzes and tests each week.

Stephie isn't particularly worried about her grades. She knows that she's at the top of the class, along with Alice and a girl named Gunnel. Of course, her Swedish isn't perfect, but the last time they turned in compositions, Miss Ahlberg said that she had a surprisingly large Swedish vocabulary, and that her spelling had improved greatly since the start of the school year.

"Not to mention, Stephanie, that you have such an active imagination," she added.

In math and biology Stephie is sure of getting a top grade. Hedvig Björk isn't the kind to have favorites, but she does appreciate the girls who show an interest in her subjects.

Miss Krantz continues to be critical of Stephie's German pronunciation, but she usually turns to Stephie if she wants the right answer to a grammar question. Stephie always knows, though she can't always explain why a certain answer is correct, and she isn't always able to refer to the correct chapter of their grammar book. Stephie doesn't really know why she should be. If she knows the right answers from the wrong ones, why on earth does she have to be able to quote the rule?

German tests are always translations, both from Swedish into German and the other way around. When Stephie does translations to Swedish, Miss Krantz takes off points for her Swedish mistakes. Still, she has never caught Stephie making a single error when she translates to German.

One afternoon, just after they've had a test returned, May says to Stephie, "It's not fair of Miss Krantz to deduct for your Swedish. She's our German teacher. What does your Swedish have to do with it?"

Basically, Stephie agrees. But there's nothing she can do about it.

Toward the end of November, they're having the last math test that's going to count toward their grades for the first semester. The day before the test, Stephie forgets to take her math book home. She realizes it's still in her desk when she and May have left the schoolyard and are turning the corner by the city theater.

"You go on ahead," she tells May.

"I have time to wait."

"That's all right. You go on."

"See you tomorrow, then."

Stephie runs back, crosses the schoolyard, and bounds up the steps. She hopes Hedvig Björk, whose class they had during the last period that day, will still be there.

The classroom door is open; Hedvig Björk is wiping the blackboard. "Excuse me. I forgot my book," Stephie pants, out of breath.

Hedvig Björk smiles. "You sound like you've been running for your life."

Stephie gets her book from her desk and is about to leave.

"Since you're here," Hedvig Björk says then, "would you mind doing me a favor, Stephanie?"

"I'd be happy to."

"Take this book to Miss Hamberg. I think you'll find her in the staff room, but if she isn't there, you can just put it on her desk, the one over in the far corner, next to mine. You do know where the staff room is, don't you?"

"Of course."

"Thanks for helping me."

The school building is quiet and empty. Stephie's footsteps echo in the hallways.

She knocks on the door to the staff room, but no one comes to open it. She pushes at the door and finds that it's unlocked.

She doesn't feel completely comfortable walking in when no one is there, but she opens the door.

The light coming through the window hits her eyes, but Stephie discerns a figure inside. It's not a teacher.

It's Alice.

She's standing at Hedvig Björk's desk, bent forward as if she has been rummaging through the piles of paper on it. She straightens up and sees Stephie. "What are you doing here?"

"I'm supposed to leave this book for Miss Hamberg."

"Miss Björk asked me to get something for her," Alice says, "but I can't find it. You can put the book over there, on Miss Hamberg's desk."

There's something fishy going on. If Hedvig Björk asked Alice to go and get her something, she could also have sent the book for Miss Hamberg with her. But if she didn't send Alice, what is Alice doing in the staff room? What has she been looking for on Miss Björk's desk?

"Don't worry," Stephie says. "I won't tell."

Alice avoids her gaze. "What do you mean? Tell what? You're always imagining things. You've been spying on me since the very first day of school. Sitting by the pond in

119

the afternoons—staring at me when I pass. I've told you to leave me alone. Don't you get it?"

Stephie hears her own voice, clear but distant, as if it belongs to someone else: "Why do you hate me?"

"Because you make me so ashamed."

"Me? Why?"

"My family has lived here for four generations," says Alice. "We've never had to be embarrassed about being Jewish. My parents and even my grandparents speak perfect Swedish. My father's a prominent businessman. We socialize with everyone worth knowing in this city. But now you refugees are turning up. People who have nothing, and who can't even speak Swedish. That makes it different for us, too. People might think we're like you."

Stephie's dumbstruck. It takes her most of a minute to figure out what she should say: "What if Sweden had been occupied, too? Like Denmark and Norway? What if the Germans had come here and taken your papa's business away from him, taken your beautiful house and all your money? What if everyone worth knowing in this city no longer wanted to have anything to do with you? Would you have escaped then if you could have? Gone to any country that was willing to have you? Tried to learn the language as best you could? And if they wouldn't let the grown-ups in, don't you think your parents would have sent you and your sisters and brothers away?"

But by that time, Alice has swept past her through the door and vanished down the long corridor.

twenty

"Stephanie!"

Stephie stops in her tracks. Without having to turn around, she knows who's calling her name. She'd know his voice anywhere.

"Hang on," she says to May. "It's Sven."

May knows, of course, that Sven is the son of the family with whom Stephie boards. She knows that they're friends, and that Stephie often borrows books from Sven and sometimes lends them to May. But she has no idea about Stephie's feelings for Sven. Now and then Stephie thinks she'd like to talk to May about it, but somehow all the lies she has told Harriet and Lilian get in the way when she wants to talk about what things are really like.

Sven catches up with them. His collar is turned up against

the rain, and he's pulled his hat down over his forehead. The hat is wide-brimmed with a dent in the middle of its peak. Stephie's never seen Sven in a hat before. Usually he wears either his school cap or nothing at all on his head. The hat makes him look very grown up; she hardly recognizes him.

"Hi," he says. "What weather! It's raining cats and dogs!"

Stephie laughs. She's never heard that before, and she pictures black-and-white kittens pouring down from the skies, along with puppies that look like Putte. That would be better than these heavy, wet drops of freezing rain.

"How about introducing your girlfriend?" Sven asks.

May extends a hand. "I'm May Karlsson," she says gravely. "Stephanie's classmate."

Sven shakes May's hand. "Sven Söderberg. Stephanie's . . . well, big brother, sort of."

Big brother!

"You sure have a lot of good books," May tells him. "I sometimes get to borrow them from Stephanie."

"Which are your favorites?"

"I like them all," says May. "Especially the working-class authors. Actually, I think I like Eyvind Johnson best of all."

Sven gives her an appreciative look.

"My goodness, Eyvind Johnson! We agree on that. He's one of my very favorites, too."

Stephie lowers her eyes. Sven lent her several books by Eyvind Johnson but she didn't get any further than halfway through the first one. It was full of insects and forests and strange kinds of people who were unfamiliar to her. Apparently they were the kind of people May understood; Stephie knows May couldn't put the books down, and now she and Sven are engrossed in conversation about them.

"We were on our way to the tram," says Stephie. "It's really raining hard."

"You're right. We'd better move along." Sven turns to May. "How about coming along with us and having a nice hot cup of tea in Elna's kitchen so we can go on talking?"

"Thank you," says May. "That would be very nice if you think it's all right."

Stephie has never invited May to her room. She hasn't been sure what Mrs. Söderberg would think of her bringing friends back with her, and she's been too bashful to ask. But here is Sven, asking May over as if it is the most natural thing in the world.

Nobody asks her what she thinks.

They hurry along the sidewalk, the rain falling more and more heavily. Sven takes a newspaper out of his briefcase and splits it in three parts so they each have a section to hold overhead.

May looks impressed when they walk in through the front door of the building and she sees the wide stone staircase, the gold-fringed lampshades, and the checkered marble floor. But she doesn't say a word, not even when, like a real gentleman, Sven holds the elevator gate open for her and Stephie. She's silent as they ride up to the fourth floor and as Sven unlocks the apartment door and lets them into the hall. Then she can no longer contain herself.

"Holy smokes!" May exclaims. "Not even the apartments my mamma cleans are this elegant."

Sven smiles. "May I help you with your coats, ladies?"

A few minutes later they're sitting at the kitchen table with large cups of steaming tea in front of them. Sven and May talk nonstop. Now the subject is social equality; they're talking about how working people have to get more power in society.

Stephie feels excluded. Yes, Sven does talk about things like this with her, too, but she doesn't have much to say about them. May is full of opinions about housing and child benefits and other things Stephie knows nothing about.

"Socialism," says Sven, "is the only solution. So the workers are going to have to put some clout behind their demands."

At that, Elna looks up from the bread dough she's been kneading.

"Shame on you, Sven Söderberg!" she says. "Putting communist ideas into the heads of innocent young girls."

"Elna," says Sven. "Don't be so old-fashioned. If you took a real job in a factory and spent your days with other workers, you'd see things differently."

"And who are you to know?" Elna asks. "As if this weren't a real job. And as if I could ever possibly have as good a workplace as I have now."

Eventually Putte stands whining outside the kitchen door. It's already an hour later than when he usually gets taken out for his walk.

"I'll go," says Sven, "so you can go on talking, girls." He doesn't seem to have noticed that he and May have been doing all the talking, while Stephie has hardly said a word.

Stephie and May go into Stephie's room. May continues talking at great length, admiring the furniture, the wallpaper, and the curtains. Stephie's annoyed and almost wishes May would go home.

It would have been better if Stephie had never heard Sven calling her. Then May would have gone home on the tram and Stephie would have had Sven all to herself. They could have borrowed one of the doctor's big black umbrellas and taken Putte for a walk together. If two people share an umbrella, they have to walk very close together, and sometimes their hands and shoulders happen to touch.

"What a wonderful room," says May. "You really are lucky, getting to live here."

The anger that has been building up in Stephie all afternoon now explodes.

"You idiot," she says. "Don't you know I'd rather live in a cupboard if only I could be with my own family? I hate living like this and having to be grateful all the time."

May looks offended. "That's not what I meant—" she begins.

"I don't care what you meant," Stephie interrupts.

Silence.

"I guess I'd better be going, then," May says finally.

"Do as you please," Stephie answers.

She sits down at the desk with her back to May. Soon

after, she hears the door to the room open and close. Then the front door.

She wants to rush out into the hall, open the door wide, and shout to May to wait, but she doesn't.

A little while later, Sven returns from walking Putte. He knocks on Stephie's door.

"Did your friend leave?" asks Sven. "You could have invited her for dinner. You have dinner at her place all the time, don't you?"

Stephie shrugs.

"Where does she live, anyway?"

"In Mayhill," says Stephie. "At number twenty-four, Kaptensgatan."

She puts emphasis on the address. She wants to find out what Mayhill, Kaptensgatan, and the tavern have to do with Sven. But if the street name makes an impression on Sven, he doesn't let it show.

"Aha," he says in a distracted tone.

Stephie isn't ready to drop the subject. "Maybe you don't recognize it."

"Did you say Kaptensgatan?" Sven asks. "Isn't that somewhere around Stigbergstorget?"

Stephie feels like screaming, "You know perfectly well where it is. You go there all the time and sit around a tavern with old unshaven men in ragged clothes. Why do you go there, Sven? Why?"

But she doesn't say any of it.

twenty-one

This weekend Stephie is going out to the island again. It's been a strange week. She and May have spent their days side by side in the classroom, as usual, eaten at the same table in the lunchroom, as usual, walked around the schoolyard on their breaks, as usual. Yet nothing between them has been as usual. May has been quiet and on her guard. Stephie has wished May would say something about that afternoon in Stephie's room. If she did, Stephie would be able to apologize to her.

But so far May hasn't said anything, and Stephie doesn't dare bring it up herself. The tension between them has made Stephie almost forget that confounded trip to the movies. While she's packing her suitcase on Saturday morning, though, she begins thinking about it again. That Aunt

Märta hasn't been in touch doesn't necessarily mean she hasn't heard.

She may just be biding her time, waiting for a chance to talk to Stephie face to face. Stephie remembers other occasions when Aunt Märta has been angry with her and when she has been punished for mistakes that, in Stephie's eyes, were smaller than this one. She's not looking forward to seeing Aunt Märta. She even considers spending the weekend sick in bed instead of going home; she does have a bit of a cold.

But if she doesn't go now, she'll have to go next weekend or the weekend after that. At the very latest, she could wait three weeks and go for Christmas vacation, but if she did, she'd be running the risk of ruining Christmas. Just as well to get it over with.

The raw, cold wind on the river penetrates Stephie's clothing. Still, she stays out on deck for quite a while. If she lets her cold get worse, even gets a fever, Aunt Märta is sure to feel sorry for her and not be quite as angry.

No one is waiting for her at the pier when they get to the island. Stephie looks at the *Diana*'s berth, but it's empty. So Uncle Evert's out fishing. Too bad; he's usually the one who takes Stephie's side when Aunt Märta is upset with her.

She heads up through the village on her own. Dusk has already fallen; there is not a soul in sight. After a few minutes, though, two figures, one large and one small, emerge.

As they get closer, she realizes the shapes are Auntie Alma and Nellie.

"Stephie," Nellie cries, running toward her.

Stephie hugs her little sister.

"Is it true, Stephie?" Nellie asks. "Is it?"

"What?"

"That you went to the movies?"

So everybody knows all about it. The hope that Miss Holm might not have said anything is swept away.

"Well, I don't think you're an evil person," says Nellie. "And I told everybody at Sunday school that, too."

"Welcome home, Stephie," Auntie Alma says. "You're in a bit of hot water now, though."

Auntie Alma's tone frightens Stephie. What if Aunt Märta considers going to the movies such a serious sin that she refuses to let Stephie stay in the city, with all its "temptations"? She would have to leave grammar school.

"Märta's knees are giving her trouble again," says Auntie Alma. "That's why she didn't come to pick you up on her bike. Nellie wanted to be the one who met you, but I wouldn't let her go alone in the dark."

Stephie hardly hears a word Auntie Alma is saying. Her thoughts are going around in circles. How is Aunt Märta going to react?

When they reach Auntie Alma's, Auntie Alma and Nellie go inside after extracting a promise from Stephie that she'll come to see Nellie the next day. Stephie walks the rest of the way home as slowly as she can, in spite of the icy wind blowing off the sea. When she reaches the crest of the hill and sees the white house at the bottom, she stops, as she has done many times before. Way out at sea she can see the red flashes of the lighthouse. It's so dark she can just barely make out the point where the shore ends and the water begins.

The kitchen light is on. Inside, the house is warm, and Aunt Märta is waiting. The moment Stephie opens the door, she can smell the fried mackerel. At the beginning of her time on the island, the smell of mackerel, which they ate several times a week, made her stomach turn. Later she got used to it. Now she likes it, though she's still afraid of getting a bone stuck in her throat.

Aunt Märta's at the stove.

"I'm heating up your dinner," she says. "Alma phoned to say you were on your way."

Aunt Märta has strips of wool around her knees, outside her stockings. When she moves to the sink to pour the water off the boiled potatoes, Stephie can see that she's in pain.

"Let me do that," says Stephie. "You sit down and rest, Aunt Märta."

"Who needs to sit down?" Aunt Märta mutters. "There'll be plenty of time to rest in heaven. Anyway, I'm done now."

Stephie takes the plate of fish and potatoes Aunt Märta hands her, along with a glass of milk. Aunt Märta sits across the table from her while she eats, but she says nothing about the movies. She talks about her aching knees and how it might be rheumatism, about the fishing and how well things are going, about the shopkeeper's daughter Sylvia, who is going to have to leave grammar school; she'll be going to secretarial school instead.

Not until Stephie has finished eating does Aunt Märta say, "You do the dishes now and then join me in the sitting room. You and I have something to talk about."

While Stephie is cleaning up, she can hear the radio from the sitting room. Aunt Märta is listening to the vespers service.

Stephie washes the dishes, dries them, and puts them away. She wipes the kitchen table, the counter, and the stove top and sweeps the floor well. In the end there is nothing more to do. She can no longer postpone the inevitable.

The vespers are finished and Aunt Märta has turned off the radio.

She's sitting up very straight, her hands clasped, her elbows on the table, with the big Bible in its usual place.

"Come over here," she says, "and sit down."

Stephie sits on one of the hard chairs, opposite Aunt Märta.

"Well," Aunt Märta begins, "I imagine you know what I want to talk to you about."

That sounds more like a statement than a question, so Stephie doesn't reply.

"Three weeks ago Miss Holm went to visit her sister in

Göteborg. The two of them went to the cinema. After the film, Miss Holm saw you outside with two other girls. Is that correct?"

Stephie nods.

"So, Stephie, I must ask you: had you been to the cinema?"

It would be very easy to answer, "No!"

"No," she could say, "I had not been to the cinema. I was out for a walk with my girlfriends and we stopped to look at the posters outside. Miss Holm came by right then and she thought we had seen the film, too. You know how she is, Aunt Märta. She just talks and talks and you can't get a word in edgewise."

Aunt Märta's given her a chance to avoid her wrath by telling a lie. But Stephie doesn't take it.

"Yes," she says. "I'd seen the movie. I've been to a concert as well."

"Good," Aunt Märta says. "It is to your credit that you are telling the truth. But, Stephie, you've been a member of the Pentecostal congregation for over a year now, and you know very well that worldly pleasures are prohibited. You have committed a sin, and I hope you regret it."

Now she could say, "I apologize. I am very sorry and I will never do it again." But deep down inside, she feels that Aunt Märta is wrong.

"I don't understand why," Stephie says. "I've been going to the movies with my mamma and papa since I was little, several times every year. We went to all the films that were suitable for children. Aunt Märta, do you really think my parents would have taken me to something sinful? Do you really believe they are evil?"

Aunt Märta gazes silently at Stephie for a long time. Then she nods slowly and thoughtfully.

"I see," she says. "No, I do not think your parents are evil. You know I don't. Now that I understand how you see it, I shall seek counsel, and we'll talk more about the matter tomorrow. You may go up to your room now."

When Aunt Märta talks about seeking counsel, she means she's going to think the matter over in consultation with God. Apparently he answers her somehow.

The next day Aunt Märta and Stephie go to the Pentecostal church together. Aunt Märta has said nothing more about Stephie's outing to the cinema, and Stephie is worried about what's going to happen next.

The Sunday school class is just coming out, and Nellie runs over to Stephie.

"Are they going to expel you from the congregation now?" she asks. "That's what I've heard."

"I don't know," says Stephie. "I really don't know."

Stephie has to stand outside a closed door while Aunt Märta talks with the elders, who make the decisions. Finally they open the door.

"You may come in now," a woman says.

There are five people sitting together around a table, four men and the woman who let Stephie in. Aunt Märta is sitting at the far end, apart from the others.

"So, Stephie, you have been to the cinema," one of the men says. He must be the new parson.

"Yes."

"Do you not know, Stephie, that it is a sin against the Lord God?"

Aunt Märta turns quickly toward Stephie. From her expression, Stephie understands what she has to say.

"Yes, I do." *According to your faith,* she thinks, pursing her lips tightly so the words don't sneak out.

"If you were a few years older, Stephie, we would have no choice but to expel you from the congregation," the pastor says. "But because you are so young and have not been a member of the congregation for very long, we have decided to overlook your trangression this time. Your foster mother has spoken very warmly in your defense, Stephie, and we do not wish to be overly harsh in our judgment. But if anything of the kind should happen again, we will not be able to be indulgent. Do you understand?"

"Yes."

"In that case you may go."

When they are out on the road again, Aunt Märta speaks first.

"I've never thought so before, but now I see that even God has to be a little flexible now and then," she says.

They go to Auntie Alma's for coffee.

twenty-two

A little while before Stephie has to leave to catch the boat, Aunt Märta slips her a white envelope.

"Here's some money from me and Evert, for your Christmas presents," she says. "Don't forget to get Mrs. Söderberg some Christmas flowers. And I'm sure you'll want to give a little something to your friends in Göteborg. And Nellie and Vera, of course."

It's a light, flat envelope, so there must be paper money in it. Five kronor, maybe. Stephie wants to open it right away, but Aunt Märta puts it into her bag, saying, "Don't take the money out now. You'll just lose it during your trip back. Wait until you get home."

Once she's on the boat, however, Stephie pulls out the

envelope and uses her index finger to slit it open. Carefully, she pulls out the money: it's a ten-kronor bill!

She hasn't had this much money at once since she came to Sweden, except for the scholarship money, which was reserved for buying schoolbooks. When it comes to pocket money, she's had only small change, or very occasionally one whole krona.

Her mind is suddenly full of plans for spending the money. For Nellie she'll buy some pretty stationery to write to Mamma and Papa on. Stephie also plans to give her one of her own German books, an illustrated story. She'll buy Uncle Evert a thermos, because he's always complaining that the coffee on their fishing boat is never hot enough. She's embroidering an eyeglass case for Aunt Märta at school. It's coming out beautifully, and now she can afford a piece of velvet for the lining.

She'll buy something really nice for May so May will see that they're still friends. Maybe a book. Yes, she'll ask Sven to help her pick one out. She'll get Vera a headband, or a lacy collar to attach to a dress.

But Sven. What will she give Sven? It will have to be something no one but she can give him. Something that shows she knows exactly what he's been wanting.

She is so preoccupied she doesn't even notice they have arrived until the boat is docking at the city pier. With the ten-kronor bill clasped tightly in her pocket, she takes the tram back to the doctor's family's apartment.

With only three weeks left before the Christmas holidays, the atmosphere at school has changed. They still have tests and quizzes, but the teachers are less strict than usual, and in phys ed they get to do folk dancing. Hedvig Björk has a potted hyacinth on her desk, and although she can't resist writing its Latin name on the blackboard, there's no question of why she put it there: it smells so nice.

Only Miss Krantz is precisely as usual, assigning a great deal of homework and giving surprise quizzes.

"Don't you go thinking the semester is over already," she tells them. "Anyone who stops working will find that her grade suffers accordingly."

May and Stephie spend their school days together, but May hasn't asked Stephie if she wants to come home with her after school for ages now. The afternoons are long and dull. Sven is very seldom at home. He comes in after school, takes Putte for a quick walk, and goes back out, not to re-appear until dinnertime. Sometimes in the evenings he goes out again.

One day Stephie heads to the lily pond after school. But it's too cold now to sit on the bench, and there's a layer of ice covering the pond. She walks once around, staring at the frozen lily pads in the ice. The swans are nowhere to be seen.

When she gets home, Sven is in the hall, leafing through the pile of mail on the table. He passes a letter to Stephie. "For you," he tells her.

She goes into her room before opening it.

Stephie!

Finally some good news after all this time. Mamma and I now have our entry permits for the United States! Only a few formalities remain to be arranged. In a couple of weeks, we expect to leave, traveling via Spain and Cuba. Perhaps we will be able to celebrate the arrival of 1941 in a free country!

Aunt Emilie and her family will be traveling with us. Uncle Arthur was the one who managed to organize it all. He's spent all day every day, week after week, going to see the American legation and various authorities, all of whom have to grant permission and issue documents.

We've been fortunate, since what with working all day at the hospital, I would never have had the time or the energy to do it. But now that the Germans have taken over Uncle Arthur's business, he has had time on his hands. Luckily he was also able to hold on to enough money to pay for his family's passage. Stephie, there is only one little fly in the ointment. You know how much Mamma and I miss you, and how we want nothing more than to be reunited with you as soon as possible. But the transatlantic journey is both expensive and dangerous with the war on. If anything happened to you during the crossing, I would never be able to forgive myself. Also, our capital has diminished, and at present Mamma and I can only afford tickets for ourselves. Stephie, what I am trying to say is that for the moment it is best for you and Nellie to stay where you are. There is also the fact that we have no idea of what awaits us in the U.S., where we will be living, or whether I will be able to get work. At the very first possible instant, we will, of course, arrange for you to come to us. Be patient, my big, able daughter, and explain the reason for the delay to Nellie as best you can. I will write again as soon as we know exactly when we will be leaving.

Much love from your papa

At the very bottom there is a short note from Mamma.

Darling!
Isn't it wonderful news? Every day we have to wait feels like a year. Once we get to America, I am sure everything will work out.

Kisses from your mamma

Stephie's heart is turning somersaults in her chest. They are going to be able to leave! For America, as they have long been hoping. A country where they'll be safe, and where no one will persecute them for being Jewish.

But she has to stay in Sweden. She won't be seeing her mamma and papa; she may not see them again until the war is over.

Still, if she were going to America, she wouldn't be seeing May or Vera again, and not Aunt Märta and Uncle Evert, either. And not Sven, especially not Sven.

Stephie wants to laugh and cry and shout out loud, all at the same time. She wrenches open the door to Sven's room.

"What on earth is it?" he asks, startled.

She tries to tell him, but it all comes out as a mishmash of incoherent words, a big muddle of Swedish mixed with German. So she just passes him the letter.

Sven reads it.

"Stephanie, this is fantastic! I had a feeling that letter contained good news at last."

He turns up the volume on his Victrola, lifts her up, and twirls her around to the beat of the swing tune.

Then he sets her down. "But what do you say?" he asks. "Do you wish you could be joining them right away?"

"Kind of."

"I'd miss you if you left," says Sven.

"You would?"

"You know I would. I like you, Stephanie."

He doesn't say "I love you." But "I like you" is nearly the same thing.

She's about to respond, "And I love you."

But at that very instant, there is a knock on the door from the hall. It's Sven's mother.

"What's going on in here?" she asks as she opens the door. "What's all the noise about?"

"Stephanie's parents have their entry visas to the United States," Sven announces.

"Ah, well, how nice," says Mrs. Söderberg. "Does that mean you'll be leaving us soon?"

"No, my parents want me to wait a while longer here."

140

"I see," says Mrs. Söderberg. "Naturally you are welcome to stay as long as you need to. A promise is a promise."

That night Stephie falls asleep with the letter under her pillow and dreams that she and Sven are walking among the skyscrapers in America.

twenty-three

In a couple of weeks, we expect to leave, her father had written. The letter was dated November 28, 1940. It's mid-December now, but there has been no new letter. Stephie understands that her parents must be very busy, but couldn't they at least write and tell her when they're leaving and to what address she should write?

Soon the semester will end and Stephie will be going out to the island. She's worried that an important letter from Mamma and Papa will gather dust on the Söderbergs' hall table while she is gone. The doctor, his wife, and Sven are going to spend Christmas with relatives in the province of Värmland, and then they're going to Stockholm. They won't be home again until after New Year's Day.

Elna is going to celebrate Christmas with her family,

who lives quite a ways outside Göteborg. She'll be back in the apartment between Christmas and New Year's, but Stephie isn't at all sure that Elna would go to the trouble of visiting the post office to forward a letter to her.

With every passing day she feels more concerned. Have they left? Perhaps they had to go in such a rush they didn't have time to write before departing. Where could they be now? In geography class she studies the map of Europe in her atlas, tracing the possible routes from Vienna to the Atlantic Ocean with her finger. Via northern Italy to Marseille and from there by boat? Or a northerly way, through Switzerland and France, arriving at the Atlantic coast in Bordeaux? No, Papa wrote that they would be traveling from Spain to Cuba. What Spanish port would that be? Bilbao?

Stephie sets her mind on a route through Italy and the South of France, over the Pyrenees to Bilbao. After that, she finds the map of the world and traces a line straight across, like a bridge over the blue sea, from northern Spain to the chain of islands near the line that separates North America from South America. She's not sure which island is Cuba, so she has to turn to a more detailed map, and she is pleased to see how narrow the body of water between Cuba and the American mainland is. Once they get to Cuba, they'll be nearly there.

"Stephanie?"

Stephie looks up to find the sharp end of the pointer bobbing about a foot in front of her nose. Mr. Lundkvist, their only male teacher, has the unpleasant habit of sticking the pointer in the face of a student from whom he expects an answer. If the answer comes quickly, the pointer disappears, but if you're slow, he moves the pointer closer and closer, until it almost touches the tip of your nose.

Stephie didn't even hear the question.

"Well?"

The pointer comes a few inches closer.

"The rivers of Russia," May whispers, so softly only Stephie can hear, and almost without opening her mouth.

"The Volga, the Dnieper, the Desna, the Don . . ."

She's memorized them. Mr. Lundkvist withdraws the pointer, using it instead to show the courses of the rivers on the big map he has pulled down over the blackboard.

"The Ob and Yenisey."

"Thank you," says Mr. Lundkvist. "However, if my eyesight serves, a few minutes ago Stephanie was on an entirely different continent. I would be grateful, Miss Steiner, if you would be so kind as to pay attention in class. If you did so, the young woman in the desk next to you would not have to violate the rules of the school by whispering, would she?"

"No," Stephie says softly.

"Pardon me, Stephanie? I didn't catch that."

"No," Stephie says in a louder voice. "I won't do it again."

But Mr. Lundkvist still isn't satisfied.

"Stephanie, since you appear to take such an interest in the islands of the Caribbean, would you please tell me and the class a little about that area?"

Stephie hesitates. Whatever she does now, it will be wrong. She may as well tell the truth.

"I was just trying to figure out what route my parents will be taking to America."

Mr. Lundkvist smiles dubiously. The pointer lands on her shoulder.

"I see," he says. "So your parents are going to America, Stephanie? And what will they be doing there, if I may ask?"

She has a feeling the question is not as innocent as it sounds; he's got her trapped.

"They have to leave," she tells him. "They can't stay in Vienna."

"And why not?"

Mr. Lundkvist's voice still sounds soft and almost kindly. But the look in his gray eyes is icy cold.

"They are Jews," Stephie says.

Mr. Lundkvist nods. "Quite right," he says. "A people without a country. An alien element in Europe. The Germans have understood."

The classroom is so quiet you could hear a pin drop. There's not so much as a foot scraping the floor or a pencil scratching on paper. The pointer feels so heavy against her shoulder that Stephie is afraid her chair is going to tip.

"Excuse me, sir," May interrupts, her voice loud and clear. "But you have no right to speak like that, Mr. Lundkvist."

"I see," Mr. Lundkvist repeats. "May, would you please explain in detail exactly what you are alleging that I have done wrong?"

"You have no right, sir, to speak ill of Stephanie's parents. It is not their fault they have to flee their country. The Germans are the ones who are forcing them to leave, and it's wrong of you to defend them, sir."

"Are you quite finished now, May?" Mr. Lundkvist's voice is harsh. "In that case you may now go out into the hall. And count on it, May, there will be consequences of your behavior."

May stands up, putting her atlas away.

Suddenly Stephie is no longer frightened. She feels happy, and proud that May is her friend.

"If May is leaving the classroom, so am I," she says, standing up.

"Sit down, Stephanie!" Mr. Lundkvist roars.

But Stephanie does not obey. She and May walk to the door together. She can feel that the class is on her side. The other girls give her encouraging looks, and most of them nod as she passes.

Alice, however, doesn't look up. She's staring down at the top of her desk, pale and scared.

"Stephanie, this is going to be worst for you," Mr. Lundkvist says behind her.

Stephie pulls the door closed behind them. The hall is empty and silent.

"I apologize," Stephie says to May. "I'm so sorry I treated you badly that day in my room. I didn't think you could understand."

"It's all right," May says. "I wish you could be with your

146

parents again." She gives Stephie's hand a squeeze. "Did you see the look on his face? He thinks he can intimidate us into obedience with that pointer of his and his nasty attitude."

"What do you think will happen now?"

"I suppose we'll get a detention," says May. "But it was worth it, wasn't it?"

"Yes," Stephie answers, "it sure was."

twenty-four

The department store windows are beautiful at Christmastime, full of Santas and decorated trees, garlands and bright glass ornaments. It's a pleasure just to window-shop, but with a ten-kronor Christmas bill in her pocket for presents, it's even more delightful. Stephie buys the stationery for Nellie, the thermos for Uncle Evert, and a piece of velvet to line Aunt Märta's eyeglass case with. For Vera she finds a green silk headband that will look really nice in her red hair. Finally she buys May a book. But she hasn't yet found a Christmas present for Sven. The right one—the one that will make him understand that she knows exactly what he's been wanting. Soon the shops will close and it will be too late. Tomorrow is the last day of school, and when that's over, she'll be taking the boat out to the island. In her pocket she still has two kronor, a fifty-öre coin, and two twenty-five-öre coins. It has to be enough for a present for Sven and a Christmas bouquet for Mrs. Söderberg.

The shop assistants are already beginning to let out the last customers before locking the doors. It's really almost too late.

Suddenly Stephie sees it, in a shop window she didn't notice before. It's on a bed of blue satin, and it's all of one piece, made of some ivory-looking material, with a sharp point and a patterned carved handle. A letter opener Sven can use to separate the pages of new books.

The perfect present for him!

She tries the door, but it's already locked. In the dim light inside, she sees someone walking around. She knocks, at first gently, then harder.

The face of an elderly gray-haired man appears at the glass of the door. He shakes his head, his mouth forming words Stephie can't hear. But she knows what he's saying: "We're closed."

"Oh, please," she cries, not knowing whether he can hear her. "Please let me in."

The man sighs and turns the key in the lock. He opens the door a crack, peering out.

"We're closed, young lady."

"I just wanted . . . Couldn't I please . . ." The words stick in Stephie's throat. "Please, the letter opener. The one in the window."

"You want to buy that opener?" the man asks with such

a heavy accent it sounds like he's saying, "You want a boy ze obener?"

"Oh, yes, please."

"Well, come in."

The narrow shop is chockablock with merchandise. Stephie can't see much in the dusky light, except for the gleam from brass objects and highly polished wood. The air is heavy with a sweet smell.

The man opens the grille that separates the shop window from the inside of the store, and puts in a hand.

"This one?"

He sets the opener on the counter in front of her. She touches the sharp edge carefully, then lets her finger follow the intricate carved pattern on the handle.

"It's beautiful," she says.

"It's real ivory," the man tells her. "The price is three kronor."

"Three kronor?"

She would never have dreamed it was so expensive. Her fingers clutch the coins in her pocket. If only she had seen it before she bought all the other presents, she could have been more economical with some of them.

"Don't you have any money?"

"Yes, but not enough."

As he's about to replace the opener on the blue satin, she says, "I have two seventy-five. Could you sell it to me for two seventy-five?"

"Aren't you the nervy one?" the man asks. "You come

150

after closing time and then try to bargain me down." He doesn't look angry, though, and seems to be teasing. "Who's the opener for?"

"Sven," she says.

"And who's Sven? Your brother?"

"No, my . . . friend. He needs it to separate the pages of his books."

The man nods thoughtfully.

"He needs it, you say? Well, I guess he'd better have it, then. We'll say two seventy-five."

He wraps the opener for her in holiday wrapping covered with brown paper and a red ribbon. While Stephie is putting her coins on the counter, the man asks her, "Where are you from?"

"Vienna."

"I'm from Vilnius," the man tells her, "Lithuania. God bless you."

The twenty-five öre she has left is just enough for a little basket of red Christmas tulips for Mrs. Söderberg.

◊　◊　◊

When Sven stops in at her room later in the evening, she has all her presents stacked up on the desk.

"Quite a pile," he comments.

"Isn't it?"

"I'm not celebrating Christmas this year. I've told Mamma and Papa I'm not going to Värmland with them."

"Goodness, why not?"

"Don't you see? How can people celebrate a holiday about peace on earth when the world is in flames? It's so hypocritical. I'm going to donate the money I would have spent on Christmas presents to the refugee aid fund."

A long silence. Sven twirls a pen he picked up from the desk distractedly. She's got to say something; otherwise he'll just go back into his own room.

"So what *are* you going to do during the vacation?" she asks. "Since you're not going along to Värmland."

"Nothing special. Stay home. Study, which I need to do. Read. Take care of Putte so he doesn't have to go with them. He hates train travel."

"Won't it be boring for you to be all alone for so long? Everybody else will be celebrating Christmas with their families."

Sven gazes at her. A little twitch at the corner of his mouth makes him look amused, as if he knows she's worrying about him.

"I don't mind at all," he says. "I'll have Putte to keep me company."

◊　◊　◊

The next day the whole school assembles in the auditorium. The school chorus sings and the principal addresses the girls. One of the older pupils reads a poem. Then everyone goes to their classrooms to get their report cards.

Hedvig Björk calls them up to her desk one by one, in alphabetical order. Stephie is fourth to last on the class list. When it's finally her turn, she immediately looks at her grades. Top marks in math, biology, and art. Nearly the highest grade in most of her other subjects, but in German she only gets a pass.

Hedvig Björk thanks the class for a good semester and wishes them all happy holidays and a pleasant vacation.

In the hall the girls exchange Christmas cards and presents and compare their grades.

"What did you get in math?" Alice asks Stephie, clearly trying to sound nonchalant.

"An A."

"Me too. What about German?"

"Just a C. And you?"

"An A," Alice announces.

It's not as if Stephie begrudges Alice her grade. She wouldn't have been envious if Alice had done better than she had in math, or in any other subject, for that matter. But in German! Stephie knows that's not fair. Miss Krantz just doesn't like her, and no matter how well Stephie does, her teacher will always find something to criticize.

Stephie gives May her Christmas present, and May gives her a little package in return.

"Have a merry Christmas," says May. "See you in the new year."

The first week in January, May is coming to visit Stephie on the island. She'll stay for three days.

"It's going to be so much fun," Stephie says. "I'll show you everything. And you'll get to know Vera and Nellie."

They walk partway together, as usual. When they get to May's tram stop, Stephie is thinking about how much she's going to miss her, even though they'll see each other in only two weeks.

When Stephie gets to the Söderbergs' apartment, she goes up to her room to change. Her suitcase is packed, and the boat is leaving in an hour. Sven isn't home. The long, thin package with his letter opener is still on her desk. She takes a piece of paper and writes.

> *For Sven*
>   *This isn't because it's Christmas, but just because . . .*

She stops. What should she write . . . *because I love you?* No, she doesn't dare. Instead, she concludes:

>   *. . . you need it for your books.*

She tapes the note to the present and hangs it on his door handle by the ribbon as she leaves.

twenty-five

The island is shrouded in ice and snow. Even though Aunt Märta and Stephie feed the wood-burning furnace in the basement until it's full at bedtime, there are still frost roses on the windows when they wake up in the mornings.

"If this goes on," Aunt Märta says, "this winter is likely to be even more bitterly cold than the last one."

And the colder it gets, the more Aunt Märta's knees ache. She can just barely climb up on the footstool, and there is no way she can get down on her knees. It therefore falls to Stephie to scrub the floors and hang up the newly ironed Christmas curtains. The house smells lovely, of detergent and fresh bread.

Preparing for Christmas is a time-consuming business,

and in the evenings Stephie and Vera go sledding on the hill by the school. When she gets home, cheeks rosy and coat snowy, she is so tired she drops right into bed and is asleep as soon as her head hits the pillow. She barely has time to think about Mamma and Papa's travels. But once Christmas is over, the presents opened and most of the Christmas food consumed, she starts to worry again. Have they left? Where are they? Why haven't they written?

In the end she asks Aunt Märta if she can phone the Söderbergs' apartment and ask if there is a letter waiting for her.

Elna answers.

Stephie asks to speak with Sven. If a letter has arrived, she'll ask him to open it and read it to her over the phone.

"Sven?" asks Elna. "He's not here. I think he went to the country place of a classmate. And he took the dog along. I don't know when he'll be back."

Strange, Stephie thinks. Sven told her he was going to be staying home with Putte. He must have been bored after all.

"Are there any letters for me?"

"If you'll wait, I'll look."

In a couple of minutes, Elna returns to the telephone.

"Nothing but a postcard with Christmas greetings from a Hedvig Björk."

"Elna," says Stephie, "if I get a letter while I'm still away, would you mind forwarding it here? It's very important."

"Well, I suppose," Elna replies.

Stephie gives her Aunt Märta and Uncle Evert's address, thanks her, and hangs up.

It was nice of Hedvig Björk to send her a card, anyway. Stephie wonders if she sent one to every girl in the class, or just to her.

After Christmas, the temperature falls, and the sea begins to freeze over. First the shallow coves turn to ice, and then the ice spreads. Soon there are just a few strips of open water where the currents are strongest.

They spend New Year's Eve at Auntie Alma and Uncle Sigurd's, but there is no real celebration. It is as if the war is keeping them all from being hopeful about the future. The only ones who are excited are Elsa and John, Auntie Alma's little ones, but they have to go to bed at nine.

Stephie and Nellie are allowed to stay up and hear the ringing in of the new year on the radio. They sleep over; it's too cold and dark to make the long walk home so late. Aunt Märta and Uncle Evert get the guest room, while Stephie and Nellie sleep head to foot in Nellie's bed.

"Ow, stop kicking!"

"I'm not. And you're tickling me."

"Hold on," Nellie says, diving under the blanket. A moment later she appears at Stephie's end of the bed, warm and disheveled.

"This is better," she says, settling in next to her sister.

Stephie sits up, stretches for Nellie's pillow, and gives it to her.

"Stephie?"

"What?"

"Do you think Mamma and Papa celebrated New Year's Eve tonight, too?"

"I'm sure they did."

"Do you think they thought about us?"

"Oh, yes," says Stephie. "Wherever they are and whatever they are doing, I know they're thinking about us."

But when Nellie has fallen asleep, curled up against her, Stephie lies awake wondering why, why, why no letter has arrived.

On New Year's Day, she phones again. Maybe the letter came and Elna forgot to forward it.

She'd also like to wish Sven a happy new year. But although she lets the phone ring and ring, no one answers.

◇ ◇ ◇

The snow is squeaky under the soles of her boots when she goes to the boat to meet May. Aunt Märta has tied a heavy shawl over Stephie's coat. Stephie protested, but once she was out in the cold, she was glad to have it on.

It's a strange feeling, being at the boat to meet a visitor, when she's accustomed to being the one who is met.

She can see the trail of white smoke long before the steamboat itself is visible. Eventually it rounds the point of the nearest island and heads for the harbor. Stephie stands on the dock in the wind, shivering with cold.

Even before the gangway has been put out, May is on the foredeck waving, and she's the first passenger to disembark. Not that many people come out to the island at this time of year, but there are some islanders aboard who appear to be returning from new year's celebrations elsewhere.

"Oh, it's beautiful here," says May. "I feel like I'm in a fairy tale."

Stephie looks around. The snow is gleaming, glaringly white in the sun, and shades of blue where there are shadows. Transparent icicles are hanging from the shingles of the boathouses. The wind is singing in the rigging of the boats. She's pleased the island is at its prettiest for May's arrival.

"I'm so glad you're here!" she says. "Let me take your suitcase."

But May only has a rucksack, and she doesn't want to take it off her back.

"It's keeping me warm."

They walk through the village. Stephie points things out, keeping up a running commentary.

"That's where Uncle Evert's boat is docked when they're in port. She's the *Diana*. Over there are the school and the shop. And there's the Pentecostal church." That reminds Stephie about something. "May," she adds, "I want you to promise me one thing."

"What?"

"Please don't tell Aunt Märta you don't believe in God. If you do, she might not think you are a suitable friend for me."

159

May laughs. "What do you think I'm like, anyway? Do you think I tell everybody I meet absolutely everything about myself? I won't say an improper word to your aunt Märta. I promise."

The sledding hill is full of children. Stephie sees Vera's red hair as she pulls her sled up. Stephie waves, but Vera doesn't seem to see her.

"This is where my little sister lives," Stephie says when they pass Auntie Alma's yellow house.

"Why don't you live together? I mean, here on the island?"

"There wasn't a family who could take both of us in."

"I don't understand that," says May. "Every family has a house of their own out here; you'd think they had plenty of space."

When they reach the crest of the hill, Stephie stops, as she always does. May gasps.

"I never imagined it was so enormous—the sea, I mean."

In front of their eyes the sea is endless—green ice near the shore, dark blue water farther out, and with the clear blue sky arching over it all. Snow-covered skerries rise out of the water like the backs of enormous whales.

"You know," says May, "when I see all this, I can actually almost understand why some people can believe in God."

twenty-six

In spite of May's promise not to say anything to Aunt Märta about God, Stephie is still uneasy about what their first meeting will be like. She's worried that Aunt Märta will consider May pushy and disrespectful of her elders, and that May will see Aunt Märta as rigid and strict.

But although they're different, Stephie thinks as she and May walk down the hill, May and Aunt Märta have much in common: they are equally honest, courageous, and dependable. Both of them know what they want, and neither cares what others might think or say.

Stephie wishes she were more like them. She'd like to be spared her insecurity and her doubts. She'd like not to spend so much time brooding, and not to be always trying to adapt to others. She'd like not to be afraid.

"Come in," she says, opening the front door for May.

Things go better than she dared to hope. May introduces herself in a well-mannered way and thanks Aunt Märta for inviting her. She wipes her shoes carefully before stepping on Aunt Märta's newly washed hall floor. She eats a hearty meal, but not greedily, and she answers Aunt Märta's questions politely.

Aunt Märta listens with interest to May's chatter about her younger brothers and sisters, about school and their teachers and the boat trip out. May's stories make her smile.

After dinner, May offers to wash the dishes. Aunt Märta declines, saying, "Of course not. You are a guest in our house." So they compromise: Stephie will wash and May will dry.

By the time they're done, dark has fallen. Stephie and May decide to spend the evening inside. They get a mattress from the attic and make a bed for May on the floor of Stephie's room.

"What a sweet teddy," says May. "Have you had him ever since you were little?"

"That's right."

"I had a teddy, too," May tells her. "But I had to hand him down to Britten, who handed him down to Kurre and Olle. They poked his eyes out, and took off his arms and legs playing doctor. They even operated on his stomach, so all the sawdust ran out."

Stephie imagines the mutilated teddy bear, and the thought gives her goose bumps even though they're only talking about a stuffed animal.

"Isn't it awful?" May laughs.

They're sitting in Stephie's bed in their nightgowns. May picks up Stephie's old teddy.

"You stay away from naughty boys," she warns him. "Watch out or there will be nothing left of you but your fur!"

Stephie laughs, too, now.

"Well, he doesn't have all that much fur left, either. I wore it all off hugging him when I was little."

"By the way, I bumped into Sven the other day," May says.

"You did? Where?"

"On Kaptensgatan. He came walking along early one morning, and he had the dog with him. Strange place to take a dog for a walk."

For a moment, Stephie considers telling May about having seen Sven in Mayhill before. She might be able to figure out what he's doing there all the time. But May has already continued.

"I told him I was coming out to visit you, and he asked me to say hello and to thank you for the non-Christmas present. What was that all about?"

Stephie tells her the whole story about the letter opener, and about Sven's not wanting to celebrate Christmas. Afterward it doesn't feel right to start talking again about what Sven was doing on Kaptensgatan, as if she would be making too much of the matter if she brought it back up.

Still, she can't get Sven off her mind.

"May?" Stephie whispers when they've turned out the light and May has moved down to her mattress.

"Mmmhmm?"

"What do you think of Sven?"

"He's all right, I guess."

All right! How could anyone have such cool feelings about someone like Sven? Stephie feels a little annoyed with May and doesn't say any more.

After a while, May speaks up. "Why did you ask me that?"

"No special reason."

"Are you angry?"

"No."

"Want to talk some more, or should we go to sleep?"

"Let's sleep. Good night."

"Good night."

May falls asleep almost instantly. When Stephie hears her tranquil breathing, she has second thoughts. Oh, how she would love to talk to someone about her feelings for Sven. She feels as if she could explode from keeping them inside.

May is her best school friend and the person she ought to talk to. If only she hadn't gotten herself entangled in a web of lies!

After some time, she falls asleep and dreams she's looking for Sven in a house with hundreds of rooms.

◊   ◊   ◊

The next day is bright and sunny. They take Stephie's red sled with them to the big hill by the school. Nellie's there, and she and May hit it off right away.

"May, May," shouts Nellie. "Look, I'm going down the steep part!"

There's no sign of Vera. Then, just when Stephie and May are on their way down the very steepest side, another sled approaches from behind at high speed. Stephie is steering and can't possibly turn around. The other sled swerves closer, only a foot or so away. Stephie has to turn out of its path, and she and May end up in a snowdrift. Lying there, they watch Vera continue down the hill, her red hair flying.

"Who was that?" May asks. "What did she do that for?"

"Vera," says Stephie.

"Your friend?"

"That's her."

By the time they've gotten to their feet, brushed all the snow off themselves, and made their way down to the bottom of the hill, Vera is halfway up again. By the time they get up, she's already on her way down.

After a while, Stephie waits at the bottom for Vera, who has to come down again to get home. May sleds down once with Nellie in front of her.

"What did you do that for?" Stephie asks when Vera comes to a halt in front of her.

"Do what?"

"You squeezed us into the drift."

"Sorry," Vera says, but Stephie can see she doesn't mean it.

"Wait a minute so I can introduce you to May."

"No time," says Vera. "I've got to get home."

She walks off, pulling her sled.

Stephie's angry. If Vera has made up her mind not to have anything to do with May, Stephie's not going to go out of her way to persuade her.

Two days later, though, after she has walked May to the boat, Stephie goes to Vera's.

"Is she gone now?" Vera asks. "The girl from the city?"

"Yes," says Stephie.

"Good."

That's their whole discussion about May's visit.

twenty-seven

The letter arrives on the second-to-last day of Christmas vacation, the day before Stephie is due back in Göteborg. Uncle Evert picked it up when he was seeing to the *Diana*.

"I just happened to stop in at the post office," he says. "That turned out to be lucky. Otherwise it would have ended up lying there until after you left."

Stephie takes the long, thin envelope from him. The address in Göteborg, care of Söderberg, has been crossed out, and next to it someone has written *Please forward to* and the address to the island.

But what grabs Stephie's attention is not so much the address as the stamp. It's not American; it's not even Spanish or Cuban. The picture on the little brown square with toothed edges is of Hitler standing at a podium. Under the picture is the text *Deutsches Reich* in angular Gothic print. Peering closely, Stephie manages to read the postmark: *Vienna, December 23, 1940.*

They're still there.

They didn't get out.

"What is it?" asks Uncle Evert. "Is something wrong?"

"This letter was mailed in Vienna," Stephie tells him.

Uncle Evert looks concerned. "Open it, for heaven's sake. No matter what it says, it can't be worse than the uncertainty."

He passes her his pocketknife. With trembling hands Stephie opens the envelope and unfolds the single sheet of thin paper.

Dearest little Stephie,

Unfortunately, I have bad news. We were meant to depart the day before yesterday, but as you see we are still here. Mamma fell suddenly ill on Sunday and had to be hospitalized. It's double pneumonia, so you'll understand that she couldn't possibly make the trip. As far as the other doctors and I can determine, there is no risk that she will not recover, but she was already weak, having worked so hard for so long, and without enough to eat, so she will need to stay in the hospital for some time.

Therefore, I can tell you very little about the future right now. I don't know whether it will be possible for us to renew our visas and leave, or what will happen if we cannot. I had already given notice on our room, since we were leaving, so now I will be looking for a new place to live, and I'll let you know the address as soon as possible.

Aunt Emilie and her family left as planned. We hope to hear from them once they have arrived. Mamma sends her love. I look in on her as often as I can, and spend the evenings with her after work. At least we are at the same hospital! In fact, we are almost seeing more of each other now than before Mamma fell ill.

All my love,
Papa

Stephie looks up from the letter and right into Uncle Evert's eyes.

"Is it that bad?" he asks.

She nods mutely.

"They aren't going to be able to leave?"

She shakes her head.

"What about later?"

"Maybe."

Her voice sounds strangely distant, as if it were someone else's.

Aunt Märta comes into the sitting room from the adjacent kitchen.

"What on earth has happened?"

"Stephie's parents never left for America," Uncle Evert tells her.

Their voices are distant, too. Nothing around her seems

real. Stephie feels as if huge iron tongs have her by the chest and are closing. She can't breathe. Everything goes black before her eyes.

When she comes to, she's lying on the kitchen settle. Aunt Märta is bathing her forehead with a washcloth soaked in ammonia solution. The powerful odor makes Stephie sneeze.

"I guess I fainted."

"You fell like a broken mast," says Uncle Evert.

"Hush now," says Aunt Märta. "Let the poor girl rest."

They leave her lying on the settle. Aunt Märta prepares dinner and Uncle Evert goes upstairs to have a wash and change his clothes. Eyes closed, Stephie lies there, listening to the familiar sounds: the clatter of plates and kitchen utensils, steps on the stairs. She's there, but a part of her is elsewhere.

Behind her eyelids she sees a different room, a hospital ward with lots of beds. Her mamma is lying in one of them. Her face, surrounded by her black hair, is as white as the pillowcase. Her lips, too, are pale, not red with lipstick as they used to be, and she has big black rings under her eyes. Her cheeks are hollow, and the skin over her high cheekbones is pulled tight. Papa is sitting on the edge of the bed. He's wearing his white doctor's uniform. He's holding Mamma's hand and talking softly to her.

Stephie can see it all as clearly as if it were a film, a silent movie. But it's not beautiful and romantic, as in 'Til We Meet

Again, with the fatally ill woman going around in gorgeous ball gowns. It is nothing but horrible.

Though there are no sounds to go with the images, Stephie knows what her papa is saying to her mamma.

"Please don't die; you mustn't die."

"What are you saying, dear?"

Stephie opens her eyes. Aunt Märta is holding her shoulders, shaking her lightly.

"Nobody's going to die, my dear girl," she says, running a hand over Stephie's forehead. "Don't be afraid. Nobody's going to die."

twenty-eight

The elevator stops at the fourth floor. Stephie gets out, closing the gate behind her. She finds her key, inserts it in the lock, and turns it. Christmas vacation is over. She's back in the city again.

Putte is waiting by the door, wagging his tail. She bends down and scratches him behind the ears. Then he lies on his back, legs in the air, so she'll scratch his stomach.

"Putte's missed you," Sven says from the far end of the hall.

And what about you? Stephie wonders. *Did you miss me?*

"How was your vacation?" he asks while she's hanging up her overcoat.

"Fine," she answers.

She doesn't have the energy to tell him about her parents' not having left for America. Not right now.

"I heard May was going out to visit you," says Sven. "I bumped into her in town one day."

"In town," he says, as if they met just anywhere! He's playing a game, and Stephie chooses to play along.

"Oh," she says, matching his light tone of voice.

"Did she tell you we'd seen each other?"

Is Stephie wrong to sense a shade of worry under his nonchalance? Is there something about their meeting May didn't tell her?

"Yes, on Kaptensgatan," she says. "With Putte."

Sven nods. "We were out for a long walk, me and Putte."

She tries approaching the matter from a different angle. "I called," she said, "to wish you a happy new year. But you weren't home. Elna said you'd gone to a friend's country place with him."

"Right," Sven says very fast. Maybe a little too fast? "Erik, a classmate. His family has a country place at Särö. It was just like you said, a little dull being on my own for the whole vacation."

Everything he says sounds perfectly reasonable. Still, she feels that he's keeping something from her. She doesn't know why, but she's absolutely sure. If only she could figure out the right question to ask to clear it all up. But before she can open her mouth, Sven goes on.

"Gosh, I should have thanked you for the letter opener

173

right away! It's really beautiful. I'm ashamed that I didn't get you anything. That was thoughtless of me."

"Not at all," Stephie says, though she doesn't really mean it. She would actually have loved it if he had given her something. Nothing big or expensive, just something to show that he was thinking of her.

"It's a bit late now," Sven says, "but . . . well, here you are."

He hands her a little package, a square box in wrapping paper. It looks like something from a jewelry store. Could it be jewelry? A ring?

She unwraps the package and raises the lid. The box contains something that looks like a silver coin about the size of a two-krona piece. But it's not an ordinary coin with the profile of the king on one side and the coat of arms of Sweden on the other. Instead of the king, there's an angel, and on the other side are two clasped hands.

Two hands—hers and Sven's?

"It's an amulet," Sven explains. "For good luck. I found it in a strange little shop, full of the most amazing things."

"Where is it?"

"On Vallgatan."

"Is the shopkeeper an elderly man? With an accent?"

"How did you know?"

"That's where I bought your opener!"

They bought their presents for each other at the same place.

It seems like a secret portent.

◇   ◇   ◇

Since it's Sunday and Stephie has just come back, she is invited to join the family in the dining room for dinner. She sits erect on one of the uncomfortable mahogany chairs, feeling a bit of the horsehair stuffing poking into her thigh.

"How are the Janssons doing?" Mrs. Söderberg asks in her most silken tone.

"Fine, thank you."

"And the fishing is all right?"

"Yes, thanks."

"It must be very isolated out there in the winter," the doctor's wife continues. "What a hard life they lead!"

"Ah, well," the doctor interjects. "Just think of all the city problems they don't have to deal with."

"You sound as if you were talking about some savages at the ends of the earth," Sven tells them.

"Absurd," the doctor snorts. "You always have to misinterpret everything."

As always, Mrs. Söderberg is quick to defuse a conflict.

"Stephie, I do hope you remembered to thank Mrs. Jansson for the lovely flowers?"

"Of course. She sends you best wishes for the new year."

"And your parents, Stephie? How did their journey go?"

Sven looks surprised and a bit embarrassed, as if he wishes he had remembered to ask her himself.

"They weren't able to leave," Stephie says. "Mamma fell ill."

She hopes there will be no more questions, at least not right now, while they're sitting around the big table under the crystal chandelier, eating roast veal with cucumber salad.

But Mrs. Söderberg pursues the subject.

"Oh dear, she fell ill? I do hope it's nothing serious."

"Pneumonia," says Stephie, who can hear how abrupt, and almost unfriendly, her own voice sounds. But suddenly a lump in her throat is making it difficult to speak.

"My, my," says the doctor. "I hope she's in good hands. But your father is a doctor, too, isn't he?"

"She's in the hospital." Stephie gulps. "She's getting better."

"That's fine, then," says Mrs. Söderberg. "I'm sure it would do her the world of good to convalesce in the countryside. Could that be arranged? And then they can make their trip later, when she has recovered her strength."

Stephie reaches the breaking point.

"You have no idea!" she bursts out. "No idea at all! You can't imagine what it's really like for them."

Mrs. Söderberg gapes. Under her face powder, a red spot has appeared on each cheek. Although her mouth is open, for once she is silent.

"Go on," Sven says to Stephie. "Tell them. They need to hear it."

"That will be quite enough," the doctor roars. "I won't be insulted in my own home. If you aren't comfortable here,

Stephanie, you'll just have to find yourself somewhere else to lodge. And, Sven, I forbid you to exploit the girl for your political nonsense."

Now his wife has regained her composure.

"Settle down now," she says. "Let us put this little episode behind us. If everyone is finished, I will ask Elna to clear."

By the time Elna comes in to take the main dish away, the doctor and his wife are deep in discussion about some of their friends. Stephie and Sven sit in silence.

Although Mrs. Söderberg said they should put the matter behind them, it's still very much present. Later in the evening, she knocks on Stephie's door.

"Stephanie, my husband and I would like a word with you," she says. "Please come along into the library."

Stephie follows her through the hall and into the room they call their library. What is going to happen now? Are they going to throw her out? Will she be able to continue her schooling?

The doctor is in his armchair. His wife sits down next to him. No one asks Stephie to have a seat, so she remains standing.

"My wife and I are anything but pro-German," the doctor begins. "I'm sure you know that, Stephanie. On the other hand, we are not members of the irresponsible groups who shout about the evil deeds of the Germans and want to involve Sweden in the war. The Germans are harsh toward their opponents, possibly harsher than necessary, but they are not inhuman. That's my view, and I stand by it."

"Stephanie, we know that your family has been hit hard by this war," Mrs. Söderberg continues. "That's why we wanted to be helpful and ensure you the opportunity to go on with your schooling. But we cannot tolerate behavior of the kind you have displayed today."

Here it comes. They want her to leave.

"Still, we have decided to give you one last chance," Mrs. Söderberg goes on. "If anything of the kind happens again, we will unfortunately have to inform the Janssons that we cannot allow you to go on living with us, Stephanie. Have we made ourselves perfectly clear?"

"Yes."

"And another thing," adds the doctor. "Sven has any number of preposterous ideas about politics, about which I assume he has told you. You mustn't pay any attention to him, Stephanie."

"Really," his wife interjects. "To tell the truth, I think you ought to spend less time with Sven altogether. And above all, I do not think it is appropriate for the two of you to be in his room in the evenings."

"That will be all," says the doctor. "Good night, and I hope we will not need to have any more discussions of this kind."

"Good night."

When Stephie has pulled the library door closed behind her, she stands quietly in the dusky hallway. She catches a glimpse of her own reflection in the tall mirror over the hall table. The pale oval that is her face seems to be suspended all on its own in the air.

twenty-nine

"*If* they throw you out, you can live with us," May says when Stephie tells her the whole story at school the next day.

Stephie can't help laughing. "Where would that be? Under the kitchen table?"

"Ha-ha," says May. "We're moving to a new apartment. What do you say about that?"

"A bigger one?"

"You bet! A two-bedroom in some new buildings they're putting up out at Sandarna. With a real bathroom, too!"

"Amazing!"

"Papa signed us up a year ago. It's in a neighborhood built with special priority for large families!"

"When will you be moving?"

"In March."

"That's wonderful news," says Stephie.

"Isn't it?" asks May. "Still, I'm going to miss Kaptens-gatan. I've lived there ever since I was born."

Stephie nods. "It's not very far, though. You can go back and visit whenever you want."

"I'm so sorry about your parents," says May. "That they weren't able to leave after all. But I'm sure it will work out somehow. I really think it will."

They're sitting on a bench in the schoolyard, waiting for the bell to ring after the lunch break. The pale January sun is shining, though it generates no warmth. Really it's too cold to be sitting down, but the girls are perched on their schoolbags rather than on the cold bench. They have so much to talk about.

Stephie feels the amulet against her chest. She hung it on a silver chain and hasn't taken it off. It's under her dress now, so she can have it close to her but keep it to herself.

Suddenly she feels an irresistible urge to show it to May.

"Remember I told you Sven hadn't given me a Christ-mas present?" she begins.

May nods.

"Well, he gave me something when I got back. Want to see?"

"Of course."

Stephie undoes the top button on her coat, lifts the amulet out carefully, and shows it to May.

At that very moment, a double shadow is cast over

the two of them. Stephie looks up to see Harriet and Lilian. She tries to hide the amulet, but it's too late. May has grasped it between her thumb and index finger.

"What's that?" asks Harriet.

"An amulet," Stephie says, hoping the bell will ring and save her from having to say more.

"Did *he* give it to you?" Lilian asks secretively.

May looks at her in surprise. "It was a gift from a friend," May tells Lilian. "I don't think you know him."

"Oh, a friend," Lilian replies. "A very special friend of Stephanie's." She and Harriet giggle knowingly.

"It's beautiful," says Harriet.

"Let it go," Stephie tells May.

She knows that she sounds curt, and that May is going to be offended, but she can't stand the looks Harriet and Lilian are giving her, or their significant smiles.

"Hang on," says Lilian. "I want a look, too."

She reaches for the amulet, but Stephie is quicker, stuffing it inside her coat again. And the bell rings.

"What did she mean?" May asks Stephie as they head up the stairs to the classroom.

"Who?" Stephie asks to gain time.

"Lilian, of course. What was all that about 'a very special friend'?"

"Gosh, nothing."

"So why didn't you let her see it?"

May's questions remain hanging. They've reached the classroom and Stephie has been saved by the bell—for the

181

moment, at least. Stephie sees to it that she and May aren't by themselves during the rest of the afternoon breaks. But she has a feeling May is giving her funny looks, searching and concerned.

On the way home she has no choice but to face May's questions.

"Stephanie, is there something about Sven you haven't told me?"

What can she say?

"Stephanie, don't you trust me?"

"I love him."

Now that she's said it, there's no taking it back.

May says nothing. She takes Stephie by the arm and walks silently for a while.

"May I give you a piece of advice?" she says finally.

"Like what?"

"Try thinking about Sven in some other way. Be his friend instead, if you can."

"I can't."

May sighs.

"Don't you think he could fall in love with me? Not now, maybe, but in the not-too-distant future?"

"I don't know," says May. "The only thing I can say is that if I were in your shoes, I wouldn't go around waiting for it to happen."

"Haven't you ever been in love?"

"No," May says firmly, "and I don't intend to be, either. Not until I've finished school and can have a say about things. Maybe then I'll get married and have a family. Maybe."

"Well, I wasn't talking about getting married."

"Right," says May, "but where I come from, it's not unusual for girls not much older than you and me to get married because they have to. Because they're pregnant."

Stephie's cheeks go red. "Do you imagine Sven and I . . ."

"No, no," May says reassuringly. "I wasn't thinking that. All I meant was, well, he's so much older than you are."

"Five years isn't such a big difference, is it?"

"Maybe not to you."

"What is that supposed to mean?"

"Nothing," May says.

They've arrived at the tram stop and are standing, waiting. May looks at Stephie. Although Stephie can't pinpoint why, she has a feeling May knows something she isn't saying. Something about Sven.

"May?" she asks.

But the green tram arrives, clattering around the corner. May climbs aboard and waves to Stephie from inside the door. If she has anything more to say, it will have to wait.

thirty

$\mathcal{O}nly$ two weeks into the spring term, Miss Krantz announces a test. Stephie has made up her mind that this time she's not going to make a single mistake. She'll show Miss Krantz she's worth an A. She spends several evenings at her desk, hunched over her German grammar book. Sven teases her, calling her a crammer.

To him, homework doesn't seem to be very important. His reading appears to have very little to do with school, even though in a couple of months he'll be starting the long haul of first written and then oral exams that will determine his final grades.

"I'll be all right," says Sven. "And all I want is to pass. A writer doesn't need an outstanding transcript."

Sven is standing in the doorway to her room, with Putte

scurrying around his legs, wagging his tail. "Don't you want to come for a walk with us?"

"I've got to study. The test is tomorrow."

"Okay, be boring, then," says Sven. He shuts the door before she has time for second thoughts.

◇　◇　◇

The whole auditorium is filled with girls from several classes waiting to take the test. Miss Krantz sits on the stage, watching over them. One of the younger teachers Stephie doesn't know is standing next to her with a stack of tests in her hand. No other books or study aids are allowed on the writing surfaces. Nothing but paper, pencils, and erasers. Any girl who has a question or needs to sharpen her pencil or go to the bathroom has to raise her hand and wait for the monitor to come by. Everyone who goes to the toilet has her name registered in a black book.

If you stay suspiciously long in the bathroom, a teacher comes and bangs on the door, although the only light in there is a single lightbulb, painted blue, which gives off such a dim glow you can barely see.

Stephie is seated along the center aisle, toward the back of the room. A girl from the other first-year class is next to her. May is in the row behind her, and Alice is diagonally in front of her. The chatter ends. Everyone sits quietly, waiting for the teachers to distribute the test papers.

Miss Krantz passes out tests to the right of the aisle; the

other teacher hands them to the left. It seems to take them forever, Stephie thinks, though she knows it can't really be more than a couple of minutes.

The purple letters on the paper give off a strong smell of duplicating fluid. Stephie takes a quick look through the instructions and the questions before she begins.

The big clock on the wall ticks. They have three hours; the test period ends at eleven.

When the clock strikes nine, Stephie looks up. Ahead of her there is a sea of bent heads, necks, and backs. Some hands fly, light and eager, across the paper; others are more lingering and hesitant, crossing things out and starting over again.

Alice has raised her right hand. Miss Krantz is on her way down off the stage to see what she wants. Alice whispers; Miss Krantz nods. Alice gets up and walks past Stephie on her way to the toilet. Miss Krantz goes back to the stage and makes a note in her black book. Stephie knows what she's writing: *Alice Martin, 9:02 a.m.–_____*. After the dash, she will write the time Alice returns.

Stephie can't resist looking up again when she hears the bathroom door open. It's six minutes after nine. Alice spent four minutes in the bathroom.

Now she's walking down the aisle to her seat. She's wearing a dress with a cardigan over it. Just as she passes Stephie's seat, something white drops from the sleeve of her cardigan to the floor.

Alice stops and begins to bend down to pick it up, but

186

at that very moment Miss Krantz looks up, gazing across the auditorium. Alice straightens and walks on before Miss Krantz has time to notice. Stephie leans into the aisle to see what Alice dropped. A piece of paper, folded tightly over and over again. Instinctively, Stephie picks it up. Alice turns around. Their eyes meet.

Stephie slowly unfolds the note under her desk. It's the German test, but not mimeographed in purple ink. It's type-written, with scrawled notes here and there!

Stephie has a flash of the afternoon in the staff room—the day before the math test, when Alice was rummaging through Hedvig Björk's desk.

The paper is burning in her hand. She folds it up very small again, wanting to throw it away without Miss Krantz's noticing. Instead, she lets her hand glide slowly along her own leg, dropping it on the floor under her seat. Then she waits until Miss Krantz is busy noting down someone's name in the toilet register. She kicks the note as hard as she can with the tip of her shoe. It ends up in the aisle, diagonally in front of her.

She has lost time and has to concentrate now. She writes, erases, rewrites.

"What might this be?"

Miss Krantz's voice pierces the silence in the auditorium. Everyone jolts upright. She's standing in the aisle near Stephie's seat, a folded piece of paper in her hand. You could hear a pin drop as Miss Krantz unfolds it.

"This is terrible," says Miss Krantz. "Someone stole a

copy of the test paper. Someone in this room has been cheating."

Stephie holds her breath. She wonders whether anyone but her saw Alice drop the note. Well, she certainly isn't going to say anything. Cheating is wrong, but informing on someone is even worse.

"Well," Miss Krantz asks, "whose note is this? Or rather, who took the test from my desk?"

No answer.

"All right, then," Miss Krantz goes on. "Everyone put down your pencils and clasp your hands on the writing surface. No one will write another word until I get an answer. The faster I do, the more time you'll have to work on your tests. If there is no answer, you will all turn in your test papers exactly as they are at this moment, and be graded accordingly. Understood?"

Just then the unthinkable occurs. Alice raises her hand.

"Yes, Alice?"

"The note belongs to Stephanie, Miss Krantz," Alice says, loud and clear. "I saw her drop it. I was on my way back from the bathroom."

"Stephanie, is that true?" Miss Krantz says, looking right at her.

Stephie has no voice. All she can do is shake her head in silence.

"Answer me!" Miss Krantz orders her. "Is it true?"

"No," Stephie whispers.

"Well, whose is it, then?"

"I don't know." Her head is spinning.

"Stephanie, you might as well admit it," says Miss Krantz. "Or do you want to ruin the grades of all the other girls, as well?"

"No."

"All right, then, admit it."

Stephie doesn't answer. She cannot admit to something she didn't do. At the same time, she cannot get herself to tell the truth, even though Alice tried to save her own skin by blaming her. She is silent.

"Stephanie, please gather up your things and go out into the hall. I will join you as soon as I can get someone to step in for me. The others may continue to work."

Silently, Stephie collects her papers and walks to the door. May tries to catch her eye, but Stephie just stares stubbornly at the floor as she walks out.

thirty-one

It's like a nightmare, one of those dreams when you're lost in a labyrinth and can't find the way out. If she tells the truth now, Miss Krantz won't believe her. And it would be her word against Alice's. There's no question about who Miss Krantz would choose to believe.

She feels as if she's been anesthetized. She hears Miss Krantz talking to her, but only isolated words penetrate her consciousness.

"Extremely serious, cheating . . . suspension from school . . . lack of moral fortitude . . . your background . . ."

Why? she keeps wondering. *Why did Alice say it was me? Was it because she thought I was going to tell on her? Or was something else driving her?*

"You have a scholarship, don't you?" Miss Krantz asks.

Something threatening in her tone pushes Stephie to make the extra effort to listen.

"Yes."

"Well, then," says Miss Krantz. "It won't be up to me alone to decide on this matter. I will discuss it with your homeroom teacher at the next teachers' meeting. Until then, you will go to classes as usual. You will, of course, fail today's test. You may go now."

When Miss Krantz dismisses Stephie, it is a quarter past ten. There is forty-five minutes of test time left. The girls will just be starting to make clean copies of their translations.

Without making a conscious decision, Stephie finds herself walking out of the schoolyard toward the lily pond. The gravel path leading to it is slushy and has been sanded, but alongside the path the snow gleams, clean and white.

The whole pond is frozen over. The ice is as dark and glossy as the surface of the water was last fall, but it is immobile. Hard, cold, and still. There is only one place where the water is visible, all the way over on the far side, where the red water lilies grew last summer. There must be an underwater current over there keeping the ice open.

Her bench is occupied by a young couple sitting there hugging and kissing. The girl is wearing a brown beret over her blond hair. The boy has no cap on and his back is to Stephie.

They kiss for a long time.

Stephie looks away, wishing they would leave. She pokes at the snow with the toe of her boot, waiting.

The next time she looks toward the bench, the two have stood up. They're holding hands and walking in her direction.

Now she can see the young man's face.

It's Sven.

She shuts her eyes, as if to erase the image. But when she opens them again, it's still there.

"Stephanie!"

She wants to turn and run, but her feet seem to be frozen to the ground. Eagerly, he pulls the girl in her direction. Now Stephie recognizes her, too. She works at the tavern.

"Hi, Stephanie," says Sven. "Are you on a break?"

She nods. Inside, she is frozen as solid as the lily pond.

"This is Stephanie, the girl I've told you about," Sven says to his companion.

"How do you do?" she says, extending a hand. "My name is Irja."

Stephie's paralysis is released. Her heart pounds and her head spins. Irja and Sven. She turns and runs.

"Stephanie," she hears Sven shout. "Wait!"

She heads for school, though she has no intention of going in. What would she do there? They're going to suspend her anyway and lower her conduct marks; she'll lose her scholarship and not be able to continue her education.

None of it matters. The only thing that makes any difference is Irja and Sven.

"Stephanie!"

It's not Sven's voice. May comes running toward her.

"Stephanie! Where are you going?"

May grabs her by the sleeve of her coat and holds her still.

"Why didn't you tell Miss Krantz it wasn't you? I know that note wasn't yours. I know you didn't cheat."

"Leave me alone!" Stephie screams. "Let me go and leave me alone!"

She pulls her sleeve away so fast and hard May loses her balance on the icy ground and falls.

Just as Stephie is about to abandon May in the snowdrift alongside the path, she has a realization.

"You knew," she says, turning to May. "You saw them together."

"Who? What are you talking about?" May fumbles her way to standing and adjusts her glasses.

"Sven and Irja," says Stephie. "The girl from the tavern. You knew, didn't you?"

May's eyes look sad behind the fogged-up lenses of her glasses.

"Yes," she says. "I saw them during Christmas vacation. I wanted to tell you, but I just couldn't."

"If you'd been a real friend," says Stephie, "you would have."

She wants to get away from May, away from Sven, away from school and from everyone. Suddenly she knows: she'll go home to the island.

"No, you idiot!" May shouts after her. "The reason I couldn't get myself to tell you is precisely because I am your friend."

193

thirty-two

Putte yaps eagerly from the other side of the front door when he hears Stephie's key in the lock. Usually no one comes home at this time of day: the doctor is at his office, his wife is running errands or going to the hairdresser, and Stephie and Sven are normally at school. Elna may be at home if she isn't out grocery shopping, in which case she uses the kitchen entrance.

"Hush, Putte," Stephie whispers once she's inside. She doesn't want Elna to hear that she's come in, and start wondering what may be wrong. She takes her shoes off and, still in her coat, tiptoes to her room, leading Putte by his collar. If she doesn't take him with her, he'll just stand outside the door whining, and Elna will turn up.

Putte wants to play, but Stephie doesn't have time. She

has to pack and get out again before anyone notices she's there. She knows there is a boat around one o'clock, and she has time to make it.

"Sit, Putte," she says, and he sits obediently.

Stephie takes out her suitcase and starts packing. She tosses in all her belongings from the dresser and closet helter-skelter. She packs her framed photos from home among the clothing to keep them from breaking. She removes the sheets from the bed she made that morning, folds the quilt, and puts the bedspread back on.

When Stephie lifts her jewelry box out of the drawer, she remembers the amulet around her neck. Unlocking the chain, she lets the coin drop into her palm. She leaves it on top of the dresser, for whoever finds it. She doesn't want anything to remember Sven by. Let him give it to Irja. It certainly hasn't been a good-luck charm for Stephie, anyway.

No, she thinks a moment later. *Nobody is going to get it.* She'll take it with her and throw it into the sea from the deck of the boat. For now, it goes into her coat pocket.

When the bells ring noon from the church on the other side of the park, she's ready. She closes the suitcase and clasps it shut. All that remains for her to do is to say goodbye to Putte.

She squats down next to him, stroking his shiny coat gently. Putte puts his muzzle in her lap and looks at her with those brown eyes of his.

"Goodbye, Putte," she says softly. "I guess I'll never see you again."

Putte licks her hand. He seems to understand what she means.

"Take care of Sven," she says, standing. "But don't you be friends with that . . . Irja."

Her name feels like a stone in Stephie's mouth.

She bends back down and gives the little dog a hug, closing her eyes and burying her face in his fur. Then she stands up, takes the suitcase and her shoes, and opens the hall door.

Before she goes out the front door, she has to set the suitcase down to put on her shoes. As she is bending down to tie them, she hears the sound of a key in the lock. It must be Mrs. Söderberg.

I'll tell her Aunt Märta's been taken suddenly ill, she thinks quickly, *and that I'm going home for a few days to help out. Then Aunt Märta can phone to say I'm not coming back.*

But it's Sven standing in the doorway.

"Stephanie?" he says. "Where are you going? What's happened?"

"Home," she says. "I'm going home."

"Home?"

"Let me out," she says. "I'm in a hurry."

But Sven is still blocking the doorway. She can't get past.

"Wait a moment," he says. "You can't just leave."

"Why not?"

"At least explain why. And why you ran away from Irja and me."

"You said we would always tell each other everything," says Stephie. "You told me I understood you best of all. Then

196

you went behind my back. Met her in secret. Snuck around out in Mayhill. Didn't you know I'd seen you there in the tavern?"

Sven looks shamefaced, like Putte when he's been reprimanded.

"I should have told you . . . ," he says. "I've been a coward. Irja thinks so, too."

"I don't care what she thinks! I hate you! How could you . . . and with a girl like that? A barmaid!"

She regrets those words as soon as she says them. She regrets them even before she sees the expression on Sven's face: first astonished and offended, then angry. He opens his mouth to say something, but she speaks first.

"Don't you get it?" she cries, not caring if all the other tenants and Elna in the kitchen hear her. "Don't you know I love you?"

They stand silently for a few seconds, looking at each other. She sees the astonishment in Sven's eyes, sees him trying to take in the impact of her words.

"Love . . . ?" he asks.

Against all the odds, her heart fills with hope. Perhaps this is the very moment when he will realize that he loves her after all, that Irja means nothing to him.

But all she has to do is look at him to know she's wrong. Arms akimbo, mouth gaping, he stands in front of her, unable to utter a word. Sven, who always knows what to say.

"This . . . this is so strange," he says. "You . . . I . . . You're just a kid! Like, well, like a little sister to me."

"You said I seemed older," she says, her voice sticking in her throat.

"I don't know what you've gone around imagining," Sven says, "but you've got to realize it was nothing but a fantasy. I've never thought of you that way. And you can't claim I have ever given you any reason to believe otherwise."

The look in his gray eyes is firm and cold. The gaze of a stranger.

Stephie can't hold back her tears. They flood her eyes and run slowly down her cheeks. Sven sees them and his voice grows milder.

"Stephanie," he says. "I love Irja. We love each other."

His face looks happy when he says those words. His eyes are bright, and he swishes his hair out of his eyes with that gesture Stephie is so fond of. It's painful for her to see it and to hear his words—terribly painful.

"I'm going out to the island. I can't stay here," says Stephie. "Tell your parents that Aunt Märta is sick. Or tell them whatever you want. I won't be coming back in any case."

"What about school?"

She can't get herself to tell him about the German test and the note. All that seems very long ago, anyway, as if it happened in another life.

"Stephanie," says Sven. "I didn't mean . . . I am so sorry."

His voice cracks as he says those last words, as if he is close to tears. That gives her strength.

"Let me past now," she says, "or I'll miss the boat."

He hesitates.

"You're not in charge of me," says Stephie. "You're not my big brother. Let me out."

At that, he steps aside, opening the door for her. She's about to leave when she realizes she will probably never see him again.

"Kiss me," she says.

"What?"

"Kiss me. Just this once."

He bends over her, grazing her cheek with his lips.

"Not like that. On my mouth."

"I can't."

"Oh, yes, you can."

She doesn't know where she is getting her strength. She feels as if she has more willpower and decisiveness than she has ever had in her life. She almost feels she could hypnotize him with her will. When his lips touch her mouth, she opens it slightly, inhaling his breath.

Now we will always be part of each other, she thinks. *Even if we never meet again.*

It lasts only an instant, but at that very second, the elevator stops at the fourth floor. From behind the gate, Mrs. Söderberg, openmouthed, is staring at them. She looks like a fish gasping for air.

Stephie grabs her suitcase and runs down the four flights of steps as fast as she can.

thirty-three

The sea is frozen over, covered with a thick layer of ice, just like last year, when it was possible to walk all the way to the mainland. The steamboat plows its way through a thin strip the icebreaker has opened, winding from one island to the next.

In spite of the cold, Stephie stands on the foredeck. By now she recognizes every skerry between town and the island and can predict what's coming behind the next one. Coves and islets, houses and jetties pass by.

She's on her way home.

She carries her heavy suitcase all the way from the harbor up through the village. Her breath looks like white smoke coming out of her mouth, but her lips still feel warm.

On the schoolyard of the primary school, the children are out playing. Nellie sees her and rushes up to the fence.

"Stephie! I didn't know you were coming today. It's not Saturday!"

"Things have happened," she says. "I'll tell you later."

"Nellie," one of the other children shouts. "Come on!"

"Go ahead," says Stephie. "We can talk more later."

The road across the island seems long, and her suitcase heavy as lead. Time after time she has to put it down and change hands.

At last she makes it to the crest of the hill. Below her the ice spreads toward the horizon, glassy in the sunshine, although the sun is already low in the sky. The light is nearly blinding.

The end of the world, she thinks, just like the first time she stood here. But it doesn't frighten her any longer. On the contrary, it's what she calls the place where she feels safe.

She walks slowly down the icy hill, in through the gate, up the stone steps. She opens the front door.

"Who's there?" Aunt Märta calls from the kitchen.

"It's me."

Aunt Märta comes into the hall, wiping her hands on her blue checkered apron.

"You, Stephie? Are you ill?"

"No."

"Hang up your coat," says Aunt Märta, "and come in and tell me what's going on. I'll just rinse out this floor rag."

She vanishes into the kitchen.

Stephie removes her mittens and stuffs them into her coat pockets. She feels something hard in each pocket: the amulet, which she forgot to toss overboard, and the key to the apartment, which is still safety-pinned. She should have left it on the table in the hall as a sign that she never intended to return.

The kitchen smells newly cleaned, and there are still traces of water on the floor.

"Well, now," says Aunt Märta once they're seated at the kitchen table. "What exactly happened?"

Stephie tells the whole tale, about the copy of the German test, about Miss Krantz and Alice, about being accused of cheating. She's able to tell all that to Aunt Märta. But she can't tell her about Sven.

"Why didn't you tell the truth?" Aunt Märta asks.

"I'm not sure," says Stephie. "I just couldn't. Miss Krantz wouldn't have believed me anyway."

"Some people," Aunt Märta concurs, "don't recognize the truth when they hear it. But did you say May also saw what happened?"

"Yes, but I didn't know it until afterward. If we say something now, Miss Krantz will think we cooked up a lie together."

"Why would she be more inclined to believe that . . . What's her name?"

"Alice."

"Alice, than you?"

"She doesn't like me."

Aunt Märta considers.

"I can't tell you what to do. Your conscience is clear, and the decision is yours," she says finally. "But there's one thing I do want to tell you. Whatever happens, you will always have a home with Evert and me."

"I want to stay here."

"That's up to you."

"Aunt Märta, would you phone Mrs. Söderberg and tell her I won't be coming back?"

"I suppose so. But let's wait a couple of days, shall we? In case you have second thoughts."

"I won't."

"Maybe not," says Aunt Märta. "But I'm still going to wait until Sunday to call, if you don't mind. Did you tell them you were coming here, so they know where you are?"

"Yes."

"Then I'll wait until Sunday."

The air in her room under the eaves is cold and smells a bit stale. She hasn't been to the island since Christmas vacation, and no one was expecting her. They decide to leave her door open for a while and hang her bedclothes to air and warm up on the line over the kitchen stove.

"This cold weather is no good for me," says Aunt Märta. "It goes straight to my knees."

In the evening Auntie Alma phones. She's heard from Nellie that Stephie is back, and wants to know why. Stephie hadn't really realized that the whole island was going to want to know why she left grammar school after only a little more than a semester. Some people will believe that she was the one who cheated, and that she was expelled. Others will feel sorry for her, while still others will think it serves her right. Some will believe in her innocence but think she was cowardly not to stand up for herself.

But no one will know the truth.

She never, ever wants to see him again.

thirty-four

"So you're not going back to the city?" Vera asks her when Stephie has told her the whole story.

Well, the whole story about what happened at school. She can't get herself to tell even Vera that the name of the real reason she doesn't want to go back is Irja. Irja and Sven.

"No."

They're standing above the seashore, at the spot where the islanders swim in the summer. The cliffs where she and Vera sunbathed last year are covered with snow, and the big rock they jumped from protrudes out of the ice. A cold, raw wind sweeps in off the sea.

"Let's keep walking," says Vera. "I'm getting cold."

The path down to the swimming spot is so narrow they have to walk single file.

"So what about what's-her-name? May, is it?" Vera asks when they're able to walk side by side again.

"What about her?"

"Will she be coming here again?"

"I don't know," says Stephie. "I doubt it." Saying that makes her sad.

"I've missed you," says Vera. "I'm glad to have you back." She puts an arm around Stephie's shoulders, and Stephie puts her arm around Vera's waist.

"Next year I'm going to try for a position as a housemaid in Göteborg," Vera tells her. "You could, too. Just think of all the fun we'd have. Going dancing in the evenings . . ." She laughs. "Oh, I forgot, your aunt Märta wouldn't like that."

Vera looks bright and cheerful when she talks about the future. But the picture of the future she's painting is so unlike the one Stephie has always dreamt of. She feels a stab of regret. What has she done? Given up her future, and why? On the other hand, did she have any choice?

Stephie's lips are blue with cold when she gets home after walking all afternoon with Vera. She stamps the snow off her boots and unbuttons her coat with stiff fingers.

Aunt Märta comes into the vestibule.

"You've got visitors," she says. "They're in the sitting room."

Visitors? Who could they be? Stephie doesn't have time to ask; Aunt Märta disappears again.

She hangs up her coat and goes through the kitchen into the sitting room.

May and Hedvig Björk are sitting on either side of the table.

"Good day, Stephanie," says Hedvig Björk.

"Sit down," says Aunt Märta from behind. "Miss Björk has something to tell you."

Stephie sinks into the third chair at the table.

"Would you like some more coffee, Miss Björk?" Aunt Märta asks.

"Oh, yes, please."

"Stephanie," May whispers while Aunt Märta is pouring Hedvig Björk's coffee. "Everything's going to be all right. Don't worry."

She's not worried, just confused. What's the point of all this?

"You must be wondering what we're doing here," Hedvig Björk says, as if she has been reading Stephie's mind. She nods her thanks to Aunt Märta, who is on her way to the kitchen. "Or, rather, I'm sure you realize it has something to do with what happened during the German test yesterday."

"Yes."

"Well, it's all been resolved," Hedvig Björk says. "No one suspects you of anything. Alice has admitted that the note was hers."

"But how . . . ?"

"Miss Krantz told me what happened," Hedvig Björk continues. "Or what she thought happened. I couldn't really believe it, so I had a word with May, who said she was certain it hadn't been you. What I couldn't figure out was why you didn't tell Miss Krantz the truth at the time."

"She would never have believed me."

"You may be right," Hedvig Björk says thoughtfully. "We all have our blind spots. Personally, I blame myself for not having realized what was going on with Alice much earlier. It's terribly unfortunate."

"What do you mean?"

"The way she expects herself not only to be a good student, but the best. Perfect, in fact. Her desire to excel is so powerful she was prepared to cheat and lie. She must come from a very unhappy home."

"Alice?" May can't help herself. "That girl has everything! She lives in one of the fanciest mansions in town."

"But she *is* unhappy, in any case," says Stephie. "Haven't you noticed?"

May shrugs, but Hedvig Björk looks attentively at Stephie. "You've noticed, then?"

"Yes."

"You're good at seeing below the surface of people," Hedvig Björk tells her. "Take advantage of that gift."

"What's going to happen to Alice?"

"I don't know yet. I spoke with her this morning, and we agreed that she would go home for the rest of the week. I'll be seeing her parents tomorrow evening. If they choose to keep Alice at school I will, unfortunately, have to lower her conduct mark for this semester, and I'm sure Miss Krantz will lower her grade in German. But my guess is that they'll put her in a different school. Maybe one of the private ones, or a boarding school."

Hedvig Björk takes the last sip of her coffee.

"Now I suggest you go upstairs and pack your things," she says. "We ought to be able to catch the six o'clock boat back to town. All three of us, I mean."

They look at Stephie—May excitedly and a little nervously, Hedvig Björk firmly and calmly.

"Not me," says Stephie. "I'm not coming."

"Why—" Hedvig Björk begins, but May interrupts her.

"Stephanie, don't be silly," May says so softly only the three of them can hear. "You mustn't let a boy ruin everything for you. Think about your education, about becoming a doctor. Think about your parents."

Stephie knows May is right. But the very thought of going back to the Söderbergs' apartment, going back to Karin's old room with Sven on the other side of the wall, is intolerable. Knowing that he's there, so close and yet so far out of her reach. That he's lying in his bed thinking about Irja until he falls asleep. She can't bear it. She shakes her head.

"I don't know who *he* is," says Hedvig Björk, "and it's none of my business. But there's one thing I think you ought to know, Stephanie. No matter how strong your feelings for this boy are just now, they will pass. And in a year, or two years or five, you will have equally strong feelings for someone else. Sooner or later you'll meet someone who cares just as much for you as you do for him right now. You may not believe it, but I know that it's true. If you don't see him for a while—"

"That's not possible," says Stephie. "Not if I go back to town with you."

"They live in the same apartment," May explains. "If only my family were moving sooner, you'd be able to come and live with us now."

"Would it make things easier for you," Hedvig Björk asks, "if you had somewhere else to stay?"

"I think so."

"All right. You're welcome to come and stay with me. At least for a few weeks."

"And then you'll move in with us," May says excitedly. "Oh, Stephie, do come!"

Stephie looks from one to the other. May and Hedvig Björk are her friends. They want to help her.

"Thank you," she says. "I'll go pack."

Aunt Märta makes them all dinner, apologizing profusely to Hedvig Björk for the simple fare. Miss Björk tells her she hasn't tasted such delicious fish in a long time. "It's so nice and fresh!"

When they are ready to leave for the boat, Aunt Märta takes Stephie aside.

"I miss you more every time you leave," she says. "But this time I am glad you're going."

May helps Stephie carry her suitcase to the port. When

they are almost there, someone comes running toward them. Someone with long red hair streaming in the wind.

"Are you leaving?" Vera shouts from a distance.

"Yes."

Vera stops in front of them, extending a hand to May. "I'm Vera."

"I'm May."

"I know."

Vera walks them out onto the pier.

"I never really thought you'd be staying," she says softly to Stephie. "You don't belong here, not the same way I do. I doubt I'll ever get away from this place."

"Of course you will," says Stephie. "If that's what you want, you'll do it. And if you move to town next year, we *will* go out dancing, no matter what Aunt Märta says."

Vera laughs. "See you soon," she says.

She stands on the pier, waving until the boat leaves.

thirty-five

"*See* you Monday, then," May says one Saturday in early March when she and Stephie are leaving school. "I'm going home to pack. You pack, too, all right?"

Monday is the big day, when May and her family are moving from their one-room apartment in Mayhill to the new one in Sandarna. And Stephie's moving in with them. She, May, and Britten are going to share a room. It's a bright room with a linoleum floor and blue-and-white striped wallpaper. Stephie knows because she's been along to inspect the new place.

She nods. "I don't have that much to pack. Since I sleep on the settle in Miss Björk's kitchen, I haven't spread out. Everything is in my suitcase."

"Oh, look," says May. "Isn't that Sven?"

Stephie's heart stops. Yes, it's Sven all right. He's standing outside the fence, with no cap in spite of the cold, and with his brown hair hanging in his eyes.

She hasn't seen him in five weeks.

Her first impulse is to hide, pulling May with her into a doorway on the schoolyard and not coming out again. But he's already spotted her. He's looking at her now.

"See you Monday," she says to May.

She walks slowly toward Sven and stops inside the fence. Somehow it feels right to keep the fence between them.

"Stephanie," he says. "How are you?"

"What are you doing here?"

Stephie knows she sounds rude, but like the fence, an unfriendly tone of voice is a way to protect herself.

"I have a letter for you. From your parents. Here."

He passes her a long, thin envelope. She glances at it. Papa's handwriting. German stamp.

"Thank you."

Putting the letter in her pocket, she steps back from the fence.

"Stephanie," Sven says again, in a pleading tone. "Couldn't we talk for a while?"

"What about?"

"Don't be angry with me," he says. "Come along, just for a few minutes."

"Where to?"

"The lily pond?"

They walk side by side along the path to the pond. Their shadows fall on the snow, blue and long.

"I've missed you," says Sven.

"You have her, don't you?"

She can't make herself say the name. Irja.

"Don't be silly," says Sven. "You are you. No one can replace you. I want us to be friends. Couldn't we?"

"I don't know."

"Can we try?"

"I don't know."

"I understand," he says. "I hurt you, although I had no intention of doing so. Can you believe me if I tell you I had no idea about your feelings? I saw you as a little sister, a friend, but never . . . And I should have told you about Irja, but I was so afraid Father would find out that I didn't dare to tell anyone. Can you forgive me?"

He's stopped at the edge of the pond and turned to face her so she has to look him in the eye.

"Stephanie?"

"All right," she says. "Yes, I forgive you. I was in the wrong, as well. I believed what I wanted to believe. I heard what I wanted to hear you say, not what you actually said."

"So are we friends now?"

"Yes."

"Good," Sven says with a smile. "Putte's missed you, too."

There's one more thing she needs to find out.

"Have you told your parents about Irja?"

Sven looks shamefaced. "Not yet. I guess I'm not as heroic as I'd like to be. And I'm certainly not as brave as you are."

"There's nothing brave about me."

"You are the most courageous person I know," Sven tells her. "You and Irja. She's only two years older than me, but she's been through such a lot. Real things, not just the kind of stuff that happens at school. She's had a job since she was thirteen. And you know what? She's part of a group that helps Norwegian refugees. They receive them when they arrive, and help them stay clear of the police. She's incredible. I know you'd like her if you got to know her."

Before they go their separate ways, Sven asks Stephie for her new address.

"I'll be in touch," he says. "And you know where to find me. I'd like to take you to another concert and to the pastry shop. Or just walk Putte together. All right?"

"All right."

"Are you going in my direction?"

"No, I'm staying with Miss Björk. She lives up that way."

"Bye, then."

She stands there and watches him walk away. His neck is slim above the collar of his coat.

Sven, she thinks. *Sven, Sven*.

But she doesn't find the thought painful.

Soon she'll go to Hedvig Björk's and pack her things. She has to walk past the big house behind the stone wall where Alice lives. But first she's going to read Papa's letter. She sits down on the bench by the pond and opens the envelope with her index finger.

Dearest Stephie,

Mamma and I received your letter about moving and are certain that if this is what you and your foster parents think is best for you, then it is. From here, it is difficult to know exactly what your life is like now. All we hope is that the people who are there for you when we are not are wise and kind, and that your own good sense leads you in the right direction.

Mamma is still a convalescent, but she is gradually getting better. If only we had good, nutritious food, I am sure she would soon be completely healthy. At least for the moment she does not have to work. The synagogue helps us out with a little money and will continue to do so until she is well. Until recently, there was no way we could think about emigration, but now we are beginning to, and will soon try to arrange it again.

There are rumors that the Germans plan to evacuate all the Jews from Vienna. Those who have not managed to emigrate to the free parts of the world will, they say, be deported east, to Poland. However, this is all just rumor, and we might actually be better off there than if we stay here.

Dearest Stephie, I should not have to write this kind of a letter to a child, and indeed you are still a child, even if you have turned thirteen. A girl of your age shouldn't have to think about anything but her homework, her friends, and having fun. However, in less than three *years, our lives have taken a turn none of us could ever have predicted, and you, our children, have had to grow up early.*

Still, I know that you and Nellie are better off than the—fortunately not too many—children of your age who are still here in Vienna. To us, your letters are proof that there is still somewhere in the world where it is possible to live what you might call a decent life. We—Mamma and I—still hope to be reunited with you, but if it takes time, I am asking you to take care of Nellie and never forget who you are or where you came from.

All my love,
Your papa

Stephie looks up from the stationery and across the pond. The yellowed frozen lily pads resemble spots of dirt sticking up from the ice. Still, she knows that under the surface their strong stalks are intertwined and reach down to the bottom, where they are rooted. The plants are alive, although the leaves are dead.

She folds the letter and puts it in her coat pocket. She feels something hard there. It's the amulet Sven gave her. The amulet for good luck. It has been in her pocket for five weeks, and she hasn't bothered to get rid of it.

Stephie takes the amulet out of her pocket, threads it back onto the silver chain she has around her neck, and puts it on, pushing it under her coat and her cardigan.

She's going to need it.

about the author

ANNIKA THOR was born and raised in a Jewish family in Göteborg, Sweden. She has been a librarian, has written for both film and theater, and is the author of many books for children, young adults, and adults. She lives in Stockholm.

A *Faraway Island* and *The Lily Pond* are the first two novels in a quartet featuring the Steiner sisters, which has been translated into numerous languages and has garnered awards worldwide. Swedish television also adapted the books into a hugely popular eight-part series. A *Faraway Island* received the Mildred L. Batchelder Award for an outstanding children's book originally published in a foreign language.